A Dangerous CHARADE

SUSAN YAWN TANNER

Also by Susan Yawn Tanner

The Bellamys of Texas historical series:
Winds Across Texas
Fire Across Texas
Storm Out of Texas

The Bellamy Legacy contemporary series:
A Dangerous Inheritance
A Dangerous Charade

New editions from Secret Staircase Books
The Scottish Highlands Romances
Highland Captive
Captive to a Dream
Exiled Heart

A Warm Southern Christmas
(a historical romance novella)

The Cat Callahan Mysteries
Callahan and the Horses of Hope
Callahan Goes Rodeo
Callahan in Action
A Callahan Christmas (short story)

A Dangerous

CHARADE

THE BELLAMY LEGACY
BOOK 2

SUSAN YAWN TANNER

Secret Staircase Books

A Dangerous Charade
Published by Secret Staircase Books, an imprint of
Columbine Publishing Group LLC
PO Box 416, Angel Fire, NM 87710

Book layout and design by Secret Staircase Books
First trade paperback edition: September, 2024
First e-book edition: September, 2024

Publisher's Cataloging-in-Publication Data

Tanner, Susan Yawn
A Dangerous Charade / by Susan Yawn Tanner.
p. cm.
ISBN 978-1649141941 (paperback)
ISBN 978-1649141958 (e-book)

1. Jonah Slade (Fictitious character)—Fiction. 2. New Mexico—
Fiction. 3. Private Investigators—Fiction. 4. Western Contemporary
Romantic Suspense—Fiction. I. Title

The Bellamy Legacy Series : Book 2.
Tanner, Susan Yawn, Bellamy Legacy romantic suspense.

BISAC : FICTION / Romantic Suspense.

813/.54

For Kylah, my seventh-born grandchild.
As strong-willed—and as loved—as her mother.
She could be the writer in our next generation.

Chapter One

The door in front of her stood more than half open, but Cheney Viera rapped politely on the gleaming wood panel and waited for her team leader to look up from the stack of papers in front of him and nod.

After a moment, Frank did both, but he also frowned at the sight of her. Frowned and sighed. "You're not supposed to be here. Not for another week." His expression, coupled with his receding hairline and sloping shoulders, made Frank Lewis appear a good decade older than she knew him to be.

Cheney grimaced. "I'm not. Not officially," she added, hoping against the odds for a break but knowing she was unlikely to get it.

He shook his head and pushed the report he was reading

to one side. Frank was nothing, if not a by-the-book guy. It was part of what made him successful, a large part of what kept his team safe and functioning. "You know the operational standard. Thirty days minimum recuperation after loss of life."

Loss of life. A life she'd taken. And, given the same moment in time with the same cards dealt, she would again. Even so, there was always a price to pay, a toll taken on heart and soul. "Yes, sir, I'm aware." She was also aware that the thirty days could be extended if she or Frank or the shrink felt more time was warranted. God forbid.

Frank looked resolute but not unsympathetic. Because she could detect at least that little bit of empathy, Cheney crossed the room to his desk and took one of the chairs facing him. She wanted to say she wasn't wounded, didn't need the time. But the truth was something different. The truth was she didn't want the time, didn't want to reflect. She wanted to keep her mind and her body busy. Maggie called that avoidance coping. Cheney called it moving on.

But Cheney couldn't lie to him, not this man, who'd become as much friend and mentor as he was her boss. Besides, he knew her too well, knew all of her history, even the parts she wished no one knew. Cheney couldn't *not* ask, but knowing Frank as she did, she didn't push. She waited, gave him time to consider, time to balance the rules against the needs of one of his team.

Rather than stare at him, she shifted her gaze to the wall of windows behind him. That expanse of glass was one of the many things she loved about being part of the dynasty she'd never known waited for her, never known looked for her, until they'd found her. Until Jonah came for her. The descendants of three families, all who understood the need for space and sunlight and freedom. It came down through their blood, the Bellamy and the Slade and the Welles blood, whichever it was that ran through their veins. And there was some of each in every department of Welles Enterprises. Every office in every building they occupied had a wall of windows overlooking downtown Albuquerque. Inner spaces were for conference rooms and break rooms, for storage closets and elevators.

She was grateful for what had been given her by birth and by grace and by the determination of a family resolved to find her. The blood ties to the Bellamy line were so far back in decades as to seem negligible to most people, but they had not wavered until she was safe among them. She did her best to abide by the rules that came with the privilege, but being idle didn't come easy to her.

"I can't send you back out into the field," Frank said at last, answering the unasked question that lay between them. "That's off the table."

Cheney took a breath. She was too smart to argue, but she could negotiate. "Fine, but give me something. I've been to the gym twice a day for three weeks, to the range twice a day for those same three weeks." She grimaced. "I even deep-cleaned my apartment, and I hate my apartment."

Frank tapped a pencil against his desktop, but she didn't see irritation in his eyes. She saw resignation, and maybe a hint of amusement. "Might be a good time to go apartment hunting. Maybe consider a small house in a quiet neighborhood."

"Where I am is better for work." And work was all Cheney had. All she wanted. Besides, while she didn't love her apartment, she really didn't hate it either. The small space was her haven, the home she hadn't had since childhood. But, for the moment, it represented forced idleness.

Frank studied her face for a long moment.

Her voice was just short of pleading when she said his name quietly, adding, "...please."

He muttered a mild oath as he got to his feet and crossed to a set of double doors which opened to storage space filled with file cabinets and shelves. Cheney breathed a sigh of relief. She'd won. She wasn't sure exactly what or just how much, but ... something.

After rummaging a moment, he returned with several accordion folders and placed them on the desk between them, then sat. "These are the cold cases turned over to us in the past few weeks." His eyes now gleamed with the energy and intelligence he brought to every job. "I copied them for Jessup, but something about a few of them caught my eye. I held up passing them on, but haven't had time to get back to them. There's been a lot on the hot plate lately."

She knew her absence had put extra work on others, but he didn't say a word about that.

"You know I can't give you field work, Cheney. Wouldn't if I could ... but I can give you this much. Comb through these and see if anything needs a reroute before we hand them off for investigation."

Cheney knew the cases could have come from any of several law enforcement agencies within the state. Once a case went cold, if a link to any facet of Welles Enterprises or the families had been identified during the investigation, a copy of the file came to them. Frank reviewed them first to ensure nothing his team was actively working could be related, then handed it off to the team lead for the investigative unit. Anything hinting of violence done to— or by—blood kin was kicked upstairs to Colter Bellamy or Jonah Slade.

"You're trusting me with this? You know this isn't my

area of expertise." Even so, she'd been through the training for the fact-finding side of the agency, all of the team had.

"I also know you're good at it. More than good. I saw the results of your work during your six-month training rotation. Just because you didn't like it as much as you did field work, doesn't mean you're less capable of piecing information together than the operatives who choose it for their career."

She stood and gathered the folders into her arms. "Then I'm grateful. I really am." She gave him as much of a smile as she could muster these days. "And I'll take myself out of your hair, now."

His gaze softened as he walked her to the door. "Let me know if you find any hot spots in those files."

She'd know one if she saw it. "Before or after Thursday?" Their designated team meeting day. Every team, all the way up to the executives, met frequently to debrief their lead and each other. Should a team member fail to check in, time wouldn't be lost getting up to speed in knowing where to look … and at whom.

He hesitated before answering, "Your call on that. And Cheney?" She turned and met his gaze. "Keep seeing Maggie."

"I'm headed there now," she admitted while *not* admitting how very much she didn't want to be. She liked the department's shrink, would be happy to chat with her over a glass of wine. Talking about her feelings now, the thoughts that went through her mind the moment she'd pulled the trigger and in the moments after, not so much.

Her phone, still on silent, buzzed as Frank's door closed softly behind her. Pulling it from her pocket, she glanced at the display but didn't answer the call.

* * *

"You want me to confess to things I don't feel."

"No," Maggie Byrnes didn't react to the accusation. She simply continued to watch Cheney with her steady gaze, "I want you to admit to things you do feel so you can move past them."

"You don't know what I feel." Cheney forced herself not to fidget or drum her fingers on the small conference table between them. She didn't like feeling unreasonable, didn't like *being* unreasonable, but she hated this part of her job. That it was a requirement for every one of them after any job with a fatality didn't make it any easier.

"That's true. I don't know *what* but I know that you *do*." Maggie leaned back in her chair and studied her for a moment. "Still ... something's different today. You're not relaxed, but ... less tense, maybe?"

"Don't get excited. It's not because I've had great sex since the last time you saw me."

Maggie's lip twitched in amusement. "It sure wouldn't hurt if you did."

Cheney grimaced. "Sorry."

"No apologies needed. It's always open mic with me, you know that. But, if not great sex, then what?"

Cheney shrugged. "I went to see Frank this morning, too. He gave me something to do, some files to study."

"And that made you happy? Files?" This time Maggie let herself smile. "You don't like paperwork."

"Happy, no, but I also don't like staring at four walls or walking the streets or window shopping, and I've read every current release that interests me."

"What about meeting friends for lunch or a movie?

Taking a drive in the country or a walk in the park?"

"All of those are supposed to be things that might make me feel better about taking someone's life?"

"In taking one, you saved another ... possibly several. Do you need more than that to make you feel better?"

Cheney slowly exhaled as she shook her head. "No. While I don't feel good about it, I can accept the necessity."

Maggie's voice softened as she asked, "And the necessity that it had to be you?"

"That, too."

"But?"

Cheney closed her eyes for a moment, but only for a moment. "But a bystander died."

"Not by your hand."

"No."

"And not an innocent bystander. At least not entirely."

This time Cheney didn't answer. There *was* no answer ... no way for Cheney, or anyone, to know for sure. Some secrets went to the grave.

Chapter Two

Jonah could feel his partner watching him and looked up to meet his gaze. "What?"

"You tell me," Colter leaned back in his chair. "You've been staring into that beer for a while. And that plate of wings is cold by now."

They'd met at one of their favorite places to unwind after a difficult case, and the last one had been that in spades for a number of reasons, more personal than professional.

In the background, the crowd shifted as it always did this time of day, some would be leaving for home, others coming in to avoid going home.

Instead of answering, Jonah turned to stare at the sidewalk that lay beyond the wall of windows at the front of the restaurant and bar. Late as it was, traffic on the street seethed and simmered, not as crowded as at lunchtime, but still restless. Like Jonah. He turned back with quick irritation, at himself, at the situation. "Have you heard from Cheney?" He hated even asking the question. Knowing what Colter would read into it. Knowing something was there to be read into it.

"Since completing the Pederson case? No. I haven't. And there's no reason I should have."

"So, you don't know if she's okay," Jonah countered.

"But I don't know that she isn't," Colter said evenly. "Do you?"

Knew? No. Suspected? Hell yeah. "Her thirty-day leave is up. Her office is empty, and she's not answering her phone."

Colter waited, watching him with that steady gaze until Jonah added, "Or her doorbell."

Colter leaned back in his chair, saying nothing. He didn't have to. His expression alone put Jonah on the defensive.

"You know what kind of hell the lethal force investigation put her through." They'd all been through it at some point. Not to mention the fact of having been forced in a split-second into the position of judge, jury, and executioner. A choice which made that investigation inevitable.

"It *is* hell," Colter agreed, "but it's necessary, and it would be far worse if Cheney, if *any* of us, were left to wing it alone afterward. You know that as well as I do. And so does Cheney."

"That doesn't make it any easier, and she's been to hell and back already." He stared Colter down. Or tried to. "And Pederson's murder wasn't just a case to you so don't pretend it was. You came out of it engaged." It was almost an accusation.

"And you're engaged," Colter countered, just as swiftly, "but not to Cheney."

Jonah voiced an expletive he didn't use often, but when he did, he meant it. Easy for Colter to keep his cool. His woman was safe. A quick consciousness of that thought slid through his mind, making him wince inwardly. As Colter had just pointed out, Cheney wasn't his woman.

Colter stared at him, his expression a mix of concern and frustration. Jonah understood his feelings. They were work partners, they were kin, they were more. And Jonah was just as frustrated, if not more.

"Jonah, what do you want me to do?"

"I need to know she's okay." He hesitated, before adding. "And if she's gone, I need to find her."

"Then go. Do what you have to do. I've got this. Whatever comes up. I have it." He paused, sighed. "But Jonah?"

Jonah waited in silence. He could have done without the words he knew were coming, but Colter needed to say them.

"You know what's at stake."

He did. All too well. "You mean Angie." It wasn't a question.

Colter nodded. "That's exactly what I mean. She may not be here when you get back, and I don't know that I'd blame her. But that decision is yours."

Jonah hesitated before admitting, "I don't know that it *is* a decision. I can't *not* go. And I don't know that I'd blame Angie, either. But it's what I have to do." He hesitated. "I know you don't understand."

Colter shook his head. "Hell, I understand better than anyone. Even you. And, Jonah, if you need me, I'll come. Anytime, anyway, anyplace."

Jonah gave a short nod. He'd carry that promise with him—and it *was* a promise—if only because Jonah knew he might very well need Colter. Cheney had a way of placing herself in the worst possible scenario. Jonah had tried for years to believe it wasn't intentional, but it happened too often to convince him. Cheney was still trying to atone for sins she'd never committed. And she was willing to die trying as long as it meant taking the bad guys down with her.

* * *

The following morning, Jonah found himself headed across town. He'd tried to convince himself otherwise, reminding himself that Cheney didn't want or need him in her life. Her words. He could go with the *not wanted*, but his gut told him otherwise on the *not needed*.

A little over a decade ago, he'd found her in a very bad place and a worse state of mind and taken her to the only place, the only people, he trusted to help her heal. But Cheney hadn't wanted to be healed. Or saved. What she'd wanted was revenge, and he'd taken that chance from her. She hadn't thanked him for it. He doubted she ever would because he understood what drove her. And there was something else she'd never thank him for, never forgive him for, but he kept that something pushed way to the back of his mind.

At the entrance to her apartment building, he nodded at the doorman who nodded back politely. "Mr. Slade. Good to see you, sir." Neither mentioned his earlier visits nor the brevity of them.

Jonah took a moment to chat with the man because every person who worked under the umbrella of Welles

Enterprises in any capacity was worth that moment. A close second to that was simply the fact that he wasn't looking forward to being face-to-face with Cheney in a place as small and private as her apartment. Despite that, he hoped she was there this time. His gut told him she wouldn't be.

Taking a deep breath, he headed for the elevator and pressed the button firmly for the fourth floor. Cheney had earned her way to top pay and could have afforded any number of luxury apartments. Instead, she'd never left the simple but safe place that Welles Enterprises had provided for her as a novice employee.

From the instant he pressed the button beside her door, Jonah knew his gut was right. Cheney wasn't there. The apartment was empty. He could sense it just as he had before. Still, he waited a moment before letting himself in with the master key he'd pulled from the vault.

The floor plan was an unpretentious living space that flowed into a dining area that opened onto the kitchen. Hardwood throughout, floors bare. The furnishings made him smile in spite of the tension that gripped him. The living area held a single armchair, a wall-mounted television, and some serious exercise equipment, none of which appeared to hold any of the gadgetry that would tie it to interactive software or personal coaches.

In place of a dining table stood an oversized desk of dark, almost ebony, wood. It had seen better days, but the finger he ran along the edge remained dust-free although littered with unopened mail of the mundane variety. He checked the postmark dates on a few of the envelopes. If Cheney was in the wind, she hadn't been gone long, and he'd find her.

The kitchen countertop held a coffee pot, a microwave, and a bottle of whiskey that was three-quarters full. Not the cheap stuff, either. The sink was dry and empty. He pressed the lever to the garbage can with his foot and saw the clean, empty bag he'd expected to find.

A short hallway opened from the dining room, and Jonah followed it past a large bath to the bedroom which contained a long, low dresser without a mirror, a nightstand on which stood a small framed photo, and a bed neatly made. All dark wood, again, and not new. A closet with tops and jeans on one side and bare on the other. No dresses hung from either rod. No heels rested in the shoe rack. He took note of the suitcase shoved to one corner, but it didn't mean much. A duffle bag would be more her style if she were following a thread she shouldn't be following or running from demons that couldn't be left behind.

Or maybe she'd just gone for a walk. All he had were suspicions. Strong ones. If he put money on anything it would be that Cheney was chasing a lead … straight back to San Francisco. She might be a step ahead of him but he planned to catch up. Fast.

He returned to the living room and stood looking around for a moment. After double-tracking most of high school and college, she'd been on the job and in this apartment for six years and hung not a single picture on the wall.

There was only the small one on her nightstand. Of Cheney, as she'd been when he'd found her all those years ago. A half wild child, who already knew far too much, defiant, furious with the world, but breathtakingly beautiful with wide green eyes, red-gold curls twisted into a single, long plait, and that incredible skin, flawless save for the tattoo that wrapped one arm. Why did she keep it? To remind herself of what she'd been? Or what she could become again?

* * *

An hour later, he was on the other side of the city, at the door of Dr. Margaret Byrnes. Her receptionist waved him in, saying, "She's free for the next thirty or so."

As Jonah stepped into her office, the woman behind the desk set aside the folder in her hands. "Jonah." Her voice was warm with welcome.

"Maggie." He smiled. "How are you?"

"Better than you, I suspect." She'd changed very little through the years. Her gaze was as piercing as ever. Her once blonde hair, now threaded with silver, styled in the same pageboy cut she'd always worn, swung softly when she tilted her head at him. "Is your visit personal or professional?" And she always cut to the chase.

He hesitated, started to lie, then shrugged as his glance fell on the photographs scattered across the credenza behind her desk. Her oldest grandson was featured front and center. "Rick's golf swing is looking good."

"Good enough for that scholarship he has his heart set on," she agreed. "Sit down, Jonah, please. And relax. Coffee?" Jonah shook his head. She was prepared for every visitor, but he knew all Maggie ever drank was tea, hot in the winter, cold in the summer.

He sat and they studied each other a moment. He knew from experience that Maggie's memory was phenomenal, and he didn't care for the perception in her eyes.

"You know I can't tell you anything about Cheney's status."

"I know. And I agree with that in theory. You can, however answer questions about her readiness for duty."

Maggie narrowed her eyes, deepening the faint lines

age had placed at their corners. "You have a job for her? Really?"

At his silence, she shook her head. "You forget, I know how long and hard you fought, behind the scenes, to keep Cheney out of the agency."

Hell, yeah, he'd fought. Cheney wanted in for all the wrong reasons, but she'd been dogged in her determination and spectacular in her success from martial arts to firearms to stealth. He didn't begrudge the skills, even understood her reasons although they scared the hell out of him. Beyond that, he knew not everyone was strong enough to withstand the emotional toll of the work they did. His mind had never moved past the sixteen-year-old victim he'd rescued. His body, his physical reaction to her, had—hell, yeah, long ago—but not his mind.

Maggie leaned back in her chair. "I also know she wasn't who you wanted on the Pederson case."

Jonah shrugged. That was another point he wouldn't deny. Or debate. But Colter had needed the best they had. Cheney was one of those best.

"Ask me something I can answer, Jonah." Her voice wasn't unkind, and Jonah knew Maggie understood more than he would've liked.

"Has she missed any appointments?"

"None."

He hesitated. "I went into her apartment this morning."

Maggie waited in silence. She wouldn't criticize, but he knew she wouldn't approve, either.

"It felt ... empty. I need to find her."

"Is she missing?"

Jonah turned his head toward the window and the rooftops spread across the city beyond, then turned his gaze back to the psychiatrist. "I don't know."

"Then come back and ask when you do."

"Damn it, Maggie, if she's hit the streets, I may not have that luxury."

Maggie blew out a breath. "*If* she were missing, I could only tell you—very truthfully—that I didn't see or hear anything in our exchanges that would make me afraid for her. In fact, her last visit she seemed more content than previously."

"What changed? Do you know?"

"Frank relented enough to hand over some cold cases for her to comb through. Before that she'd been restless, edgy. Having something productive to do seemed to help, to give her a new focus."

Her words eased one fear and raised another, but all Jonah said was, "It's no secret that Cheney likes being busy."

"Most of us do," Maggie agreed with a faint smile.

Jonah got to his feet. "Her thirty days ended yesterday, but she didn't return to work."

For a moment, he thought Maggie wasn't going to comment.

"She requested additional time off," Maggie was choosing her words carefully which made Jonah uncomfortable as hell.

"How long?" he pressed.

"Two weeks. It's not uncommon after a loss of life case."

"Frank approved?"

"He approved as much time as she wanted as long as she scheduled a wrap-up session with me on her return."

"Two weeks." Jonah's chest tightened. "I need to know if she misses that session." He planned to find Cheney long before then.

"If and when I have to make that call to Frank—and I hope I don't—I'll ask him to give you a heads-up."

"I'd appreciate it." Although Jonah thanked her for the concession, he intended to tell Frank himself. He also intended to find out what was in those files Frank had given Cheney.

"I suppose you're going to badger Frank now?"

"With no great expectation of luck there, either," he admitted.

Her lips quirked. "I gave you more than he will."

"Is that a warning? That I'll get less than nothing from him?"

She smiled, neither agreeing nor denying she'd given him that nothing. He was almost to the door when she said, "Give my best to Angie."

Jonah turned and nodded. "I'll do that."

"Have the two of you set a date yet? I'm counting on an invitation."

He smiled. "I'll save a dance just for you."

Jonah could feel her gaze on his back as he walked out. He hadn't answered her question, and he knew she hadn't missed the fact.

* * *

Frank was going to be the hardest to crack. Jonah decided to make his pitch over lunch in the ground floor restaurant, company owned and maintained for the benefit of employees, but open to the public as well. He'd timed it for after the lunch rush when the crowd had thinned and chose one of the booths which made a circle in the center of the room.

He watched the door until he saw the hostess gesture

Frank toward him.

Frank wasn't smiling but he wasn't frowning either. At this point, Jonah would take what he could get. Not that he had much choice, he thought ruefully. They placed their orders and chatted about inconsequential things as glasses of water and salads were positioned in front of them.

When they were alone, again, Frank gave him a look. "This is about Cheney?"

"You gave her time off … beyond the required thirty days."

"She asked for it, and I didn't have anything urgent to hand off to her. Problem?"

"Not as far as the time off."

"Then as far as what?"

"I'm not sure," Jonah admitted. "There was something in her expression, in her eyes, after the Pederson case."

"She took down Pederson's ex before the woman could take out the step-daughter," Frank reminded. "All justified."

Jonah nodded. "But never easy, no matter how justified. You know that as well as I do." But the look on her face hadn't been about the body lying on the barn floor. It had been about him. About them. About what he'd done or, rather, hadn't done.

"You two have a history."

Jonah gave a grunt of unamused laughter. "Something like that."

Frank shook his head. "Cheney isn't your rescue, anymore. She's an operative."

Ignoring that, Jonah asked, "Do you know where she was going?"

"No, I didn't ask. It isn't my business. I got an all clear from Maggie, which gave me no reason to make it my business."

"I need to find her. The files you gave her for review ... Maggie said they seemed to refocus her. I want to review them."

"Not exactly your area of the business."

"Unless I want it to be." But Jonah was careful to keep his tone neutral.

"Are you going to pull rank on me?" Frank asked mildly.

"What rank? You're Team Lead for Field Operations. I don't even have a title."

"You don't need one," Frank reminded.

True enough. But they both knew the only time Jonah's position with the organization came into play would be a state of emergency or an urgent case far beyond day-to-day operations. Otherwise, Jonah, like Colter, deferred to any department head or team lead.

"No, I'm not stepping in. I'm asking in. Yes, Cheney and I have history. I won't rest unless I know she's not doing anything harebrained."

"Jonah, I'll give you a copy of everything I gave her. There's no reason for me not to do that. But, to be honest, I haven't seen Cheney make one harebrained move. I don't know where you're coming from with this."

Relaxing into his seat, now that he had what he needed, Jonah admitted, "To be just as honest, I don't either."

They fell silent when their meals were being served and talked of sports, mostly baseball, while they ate.

Jonah put the tab on his expense account and stood when Frank did.

"Follow me upstairs. I'll get everything in those cases copied for you." Frank nodded his head at Jonah's quiet thanks but didn't speak again until they were in the elevator. "If this takes you someplace Cheney shouldn't have gone, I'll need to know."

"I understand," Jonah said quietly. But, while he did understand, he didn't commit. He wouldn't commit to anything where Cheney was concerned.

Chapter Three

Cheney sat with her arms wrapped around her knees. The rays from the sun warm on her face. On one side of her view, Monte Verde Lake sparkled in that sunlight. On the other, a wood and stone bed-and-breakfast nestled in the shadows of evergreens that nearly touched the modestly sized structure on three sides. The tumble-down cabin where she'd lived as a child had been razed to make room for it long ago. Her childhood had been good. Happy. Her mom had made fishing lures and all of Cheney's clothes. Her dad had rented boats and sold fishing tackle, including those lures. She'd loved the lake as a child. She'd loved their little cabin.

She was here to remember, here to forget. Then she had a job to do, even if it meant she wouldn't have a job to come back to.

The sun had begun its swift drop before she got to her feet and dusted off the back of her faded jeans. She slung her backpack over her shoulder. She'd needed these few days of solitude in the place she'd loved so long ago. Now it was time to go.

As she walked away from the lake, she could hear her mama's voice telling her to be a good girl, a brave girl. Or maybe it was only the wind in the trees.

* * *

Jonah placed all five folders on his dining table and poured himself a glass of cabernet before sitting down in front of them.

The first gave him nothing. A home belonging to a Bellamy burned to the ground while the family was on vacation. It should have been vacant at the time, but two bodies were found along with traces of an accelerant. What wasn't found was DNA linked to any persons on file, missing or otherwise, or to the Bellamy line.

The second resonated. A seventeen-year-old whiz kid, with a minute amount of Slade blood, accused of embezzling from her stepfather's hedge fund investors had disappeared without a trace. Stepfather under suspicion but no body, no evidence of foul play. Maybe a runaway. Maybe not. So, yeah, resonated, but not enough, not with Cheney.

The third nailed it, and he picked up the phone. Colter answered on the second ring. Because it was after hours, all he said was, "Problem?"

"I need you to throw up a blind," Jonah said.

"For you?"

Jonah hesitated before adding, "And Cheney."

Dead silence.

Jonah waited him out. Colter surprised him when he finally asked, "How long?" and nothing more.

"Undetermined. Frank gave Cheney two extra weeks so we're good for that long."

"But you don't think that's long enough."

"I don't. Frank also gave her a small stack of cold cases to comb through. One was on a guy missing from over around the San Francisco Bay area."

"Name?"

"Went by the name of Quinn. Quinn Flannery."

"Well ... hell."

"It gets worse. His family ... wife, two daughters, and son ... missing along with him."

Colter was quiet, seeming to mull that over. "Wasn't there a third guy? And weren't the three of them brothers?"

"Iffy on the relationship but ... maybe. But, yeah, there was a third whatever. Declan."

"I don't suppose you could talk Cheney into letting us handling this."

Jonah hadn't given that more than a thought or two. "Not a chance. Even if I could find her, and at the moment I can't. Kell Flannery died trying to protect her. Quinn helped me find her. If not for him—" He fell silent as his gut clenched. The hell Cheney had to have lived through in just the couple of days it took to find her sickened him. Some nights he fell asleep wishing he could kill a man more than once.

* * *

Cheney juggled a small bag of groceries and a bottle of wine as she unlocked the door to her apartment and stepped inside. She closed the door behind her with one hip, then stilled. Her gaze traveled the small but open length of living space.

The muscles between her shoulder blades tightened as she walked slowly through each space until she reached her bedroom, pausing in the doorway. The apartment was as empty as she'd expected to find. But it hadn't been. Someone had been here. Then she caught the faint never-to-be-forgotten male scent of him. The one that haunted her dreams, not often, but enough.

He was engaged, she reminded herself. To a very pretty woman with dark eyes and a friendly smile. A woman he hadn't had to rescue. A woman who would live *her* life making *his* a better place.

So ... why had he been in her apartment? There was only one possible answer, and it changed everything.

A sigh escaped her. Her preference would have been to spend another day or two putting plans into place. She couldn't risk doing that if Jonah was keeping tabs on her. He was unstoppable, which meant she had to keep a step ahead. She had a little less than two weeks, now, to do what she needed to do and return. Her life with Welles Enterprises, with the Slade Agency meant everything. It was all she had. She didn't want to lose it ... wasn't sure she could survive if that happened. By morning, she needed to be on the road.

Dispensing with her packages, she turned and walked back out of her apartment, taking the elevator to the parking garage below. She paused in the shadows, her gaze sweeping the busy street before she left those shadows for the sunny sidewalk. Two blocks over, she called a taxi and, a short distance later, stepped out near the first row of narrow shops. She went in and out of those shops with practiced ease. By the time she reached the plaza that centered Old Town, a series of small showers had cooled the air.

From the doorway of an artisan knife maker, Cheney watched the shifting scene. People, mostly locals, wandered in one door and out another. Some moved quickly. They were the buyers, in town on a mission. Others strolled, more than likely killing time before meeting someone at a nearby restaurant for a late lunch or early drinks.

In one hand, Cheney held a small bag with the hammered copper earrings she'd just bought but didn't need and would never wear. In another bag, a silky scarf, light and colorful and also not needed, nestled in layers of tissue. She had followed her usual random path through the square, sniffing soaps for twenty minutes here, studying herbs ten minutes there, sometimes buying, sometimes not, smiling at everyone, answering greetings from shopkeepers as she was spoken to.

She came once a month, never the same day of the week, never the same time. Sometimes she approached Lina's shop from the east, sometimes from the west. She sometimes cut diagonally across the plaza, weaving her way through local bands and the crowds that gathered on weekends. Lina was the last link with her childhood, the only link with her memories of her parents. Lina had left their small mountain community as so many had chosen to do, seeking a future that was a little easier, a little less dreary. Her aunt had made a good place for herself here, and Cheney was careful never to expose her to the danger that was a part of her own life.

Cheney had found her by accident and they'd

reconnected into a relationship of their own making. Lina was protective of her, which amused Cheney as much as it touched her heart. Most often, Cheney came only to talk, to listen, and she left the same as she'd arrived. This was not one of those times.

Lina was with a customer, but she gave Cheney a faint smile and tilted her head toward the narrow room at the back. Cheney ducked behind the curtain that hung from the doorframe and pulled the light string. Lina had updated the front of her shop but little had changed back here since she and her husband had inherited the place from his grandmother. There on a low counter was a small bundle of clothing Lina had gathered for her. Beside that bundle was a used but sturdy looking duffle bag.

Cheney turned to the mirror on the back wall and pulled a package of makeup wipes from the small mesh bag slung over her shoulder. After removing every trace of the stage makeup she'd applied with a heavy hand, she changed into the jeans and a loose tee cut for a boy. Her own clothes and the other pieces Lina had provided went into the duffle.

She was ready when Lina's customer left and the woman joined her. Handing Lina a pair of scissors, all she said was, "Cut." Not trim.

Lina's face filled with dismay. "It's just beginning to grow out."

Cheney shrugged. "And it will grow again. Besides, when I'm done, it will all be brown. Better if it's a short brown." Safer.

Reluctantly, Lina took the scissors and motioned to the stool. "Sit then." Lina knew Cheney's work was sometimes dangerous, and she'd learned not to ask the questions that would go unanswered, couldn't be answered.

Lina was her father's younger cousin, and she bore their family resemblance, but, oddly, her expressions were those of Cheney's mother. They'd been closer than any two sisters. For much of her life, Cheney had thought they were. Her memories held images of them laughing together as they cooked and cleaned and sewed. Cheney had been thirteen when her mother died, fourteen when Lina left the mountain. A few months later, her father had packed Cheney's clothes with his, and they'd headed out. Her father had said it was to look for work and a better life. As young as she was, Cheney had known that he was running from grief. She'd also known it would follow wherever they went.

Cheney sat in silence and kept still as Lina worked expertly but very, very swiftly. Once upon a time, she'd cut her husband's, brother's, and sons' hair. Alcohol took her husband, drugs her oldest son, and gang violence her youngest. Now she cut hair for a few of the other shop owners around her and for Cheney. Her results were better than any salon. Cheney tried not to care as the locks of hair dropped to the floor. Everything was for Quinn now. Quinn and his family.

Her hair was little to sacrifice. She never let it get longer than chin length, anyway. And she never would.

Lina finished and stepped back. Her lined face reflected the worry she wouldn't voice. Cheney slipped from the stool and turned to face her.

"You will be safe."

Cheney wasn't sure if that was an admonishment or a plea, but she couldn't make promises so all she did was return the hug. Cheney would be as safe as she could and still do what she needed to do. She didn't deceive herself that she was walking into the lion's den.

She also didn't pretend she wasn't afraid. For all her skill and training, she was one against the Aguilars three. And they were a level of savagery that few people ever experienced. A part of her hoped that, somehow, Quinn and his family were alive. Another part prayed they'd died quickly, especially the children.

Her stride quickened as she crossed the plaza where a trio of guitarists entertained a small crowd of tourists. Children clapped while their mamas swayed to the music. Cheney smiled as tears stung her eyes.

* * *

Jonah heard the front door open as he was closing his overnight case. He'd given Angie a key to his place when he'd asked her to marry him. And he had a key to hers. For a moment, he stood still, wishing things were different. Wishing he were different. She called his name and moved down the hall when he answered. He turned when she reached the bedroom and stopped at the open door.

Her glance swept the space, touching on the closet door standing wide, the small suitcase on the bed closed. Dismay drew her brows together. "I wondered where you were after lunch. What's happened?"

He'd wanted privacy as he combed through the files that Frank had given Cheney. He'd known it might come to going after her. Hell, he'd almost welcomed it. And he'd known that might turn his life upside down. And *that* he did not welcome.

"I've taken an assignment."

Neither he nor Colter were handed assignments these days. They assigned them. Rarely to themselves but … sometimes.

He could see disappointment in her gaze. They had plans with friends for the weekend. But all she said was, "I'll make flight arrangements."

Flying wasn't an option. If Cheney had already managed to get ahead of him, he'd be trailing buses and hope to God she wasn't hitchhiking.

"I'm driving," he said, shaking his head. "And I'm sorry about the dinner party. I hope you'll go without me."

She gave him a rueful smile. "No fun in that." She stepped closer and slipped her arms about his waist. Her faint fragrance wrapped him. "I'll miss you. Please be safe."

He returned the embrace, but when she leaned back and looked into his face, he knew she'd felt the tension in his muscles. "You're worried about this one."

"Not worried, no. Maybe a little unhappy with the circumstances but no more than usual."

"What's the name on the file? I'll read through in the morning. There may be something I need to manage for you on this end."

He hesitated but only for a moment. "It's Cheney."

"Cheney." Her arms slid slowly from around his waist, and she took a half-step back. "I don't understand."

And she wouldn't, he knew, even after he explained but, he tried anyway. "The guy who saved her has disappeared. Him and all of his family."

"And?"

"Colter and I believe she'll go looking for him, if she hasn't already."

"She'd be breaking protocol."

He stifled a sigh. "Yeah, she would." He could hardly dispute the point. Cheney wouldn't give a damn about the cost to her personally. She owed these people, and she'd kick and claw her way through any barrier to get to them.

She shook her head. "But you aren't sure? You don't know if she has, or even if she will, but you're packing to give chase." For the first time in their relationship, there was a hint of something … not quite doubt, not quite accusation … but *something* in her expression.

"I'll keep in touch, and I won't be gone any longer than I have to. I promise."

At his silence, she shook her head. "That guy didn't save her, Jonah, you did. And you've been trying to save her ever since. I know you feel responsible, but she's not your responsibility. And I don't know that she's even grateful."

"I can't not go, Angie."

"I've watched the two of you in briefings." She paused, took a breath. He saw the sheen of unshed tears in her eyes and felt his heart tear. "You trying not to look at her. Her trying not to look at you. I never said anything but…"

"It isn't what you think. Or maybe what it appears."

"It appears you're obsessed with her. Still."

And that was the one thing he couldn't argue.

"I love you, Angie. I do."

She studied him a moment with heartache in her eyes. "Unless you're willing to walk away from this, from her, you don't love me enough. Not nearly enough."

And that was the other thing.

* * *

Moments later, Angie let herself out, the click of the lock moving into place with quiet finality. Even with that, Jonah knew he couldn't do anything other than what he'd set in motion. Ten minutes later, one of the cousins called him.

"Cheney nearly lost me. She slipped into a shop downtown and walked out as a boy. She's good. Lucky for you, I'm better. She bought a bus ticket. I was two passengers behind her so heard the destination well enough to buy you one as well. It's at the desk downstairs. You roll at 8:00 a.m."

"Thanks, Jade. I owe you."

"You owe me several times over," she reminded.

He smiled, tiredly, still sad from watching Angie walk away. "I know. I'm good for it."

"I know that, too." And, because she must have heard the off-tone in his voice, asked, "Are you alright?"

"Just thinking." Some truth to that, anyway.

It would be a lie to say he was alright, but he would be. He just wasn't sure when. His biggest concern was Cheney's safety and Angie's unhappiness. He couldn't do anything about the second, so he'd focus on the first.

* * *

Cheney blended into the straggling line waiting to board the bus. For all her air of nonchalance, she was in survival mode, a familiar second nature. A ballcap hid what was left of her hair. The pants Lina had found for her, probably at a second-hand store, were perfect. A little too big, a little too long, and a lot worn. The 'little too long' was handy for the ankle holster where the material bunched above her shoe.

The tee, also a little too big, a little too long, and well-worn, served to hide the curve of her breasts and the indention of her waist. Tying the long sleeves of a lightweight chambray shirt around her shoulders added to that shield. She'd never be voluptuous like Jade or Angie, but she thought she was okay. Not that it mattered. No one seemed to appeal to her as much as Jonah, and she stayed as angry at him as she was drawn to him. That the anger was illogical didn't seem to matter. He'd saved her life, that was true, but two years after that he'd rebuffed her attraction to him. That humiliation had stung. It still did.

Yeah, so, eight years was a long time to hold that grudge, but she did. And she had no intention of letting it go. It was a shield to things she didn't want to feel.

Beyond that, or maybe ahead of all of that, he was engaged. She'd never touch what didn't belong to her.

She chose the first window seat available and hoped the bus didn't fill, hoped the passengers were mostly couples and families wanting to sit near one another so that the aisle seat beside her stayed empty.

Ignoring the overhead bins, she put her duffle at her feet and watched the sidewalk beyond her window. When a guy took the seat beside her, she stifled a sigh but didn't turn to look. At least he smelled like soap and shampoo. From the corner of her eye, she saw him stow his bag the same as she had, at his feet, rather than overhead.

The bus took off with a familiar but not too rough of a lurch, and the guy beside her relaxed against the back of the seat and asked, "Going far?"

Cheney closed her eyes and said, "Shit."

Chapter Four

Jonah gave a grunt of amusement and waited out the silence that followed. With a faint sigh, Cheney opened her eyes and met his gaze. He took note of the chagrin first but, behind that, the stress caused by the chance she was taking in defying orders, the dread of what she'd find when she reached San Francisco, and any amusement he felt faded.

"Why?" He judged it a fair question. Why or why not, either one was fair.

"Because you would've stopped me."

He appreciated the honesty—and the accuracy—of her answer even as it made his jaw clench. She wasn't wrong. He would've stopped her if he could have, would stop her now if he thought it possible. He was under no such illusion. Cheney wouldn't listen to him or anyone where her loyalty was concerned. So now he'd protect her.

In the end, all he did was nod in agreement. After a moment, she turned her gaze toward the window although he suspected she had little interest in the landscape beyond. He could only imagine the thoughts running through her mind. He left her to them. He, no more than she, was interested in small talk. They couldn't risk anything more than that for the present. Soon, as soon as it was safe to talk freely, he'd be asking the really hard questions.

When the driver announced they were nearing Santa Fe, Jonah said quietly, "That's where we get off."

Cheney gave him a look he couldn't interpret, but she didn't argue the point. When the bus stopped, Jonah stepped out of the seat row and back. She grabbed her duffle and moved into the aisle ahead of him.

The morning was overcast, and a steady breeze carried the scent of rain. Jonah pointed toward a parking lot, and Cheney turned from the small cluster of buildings. Her stride was long-legged, like the boy she was pretending to be, but Jonah didn't think this was the time to tell her that the swing of her hips was too feminine for her disguise. As a matter of fact, maybe *never* would be the right time to voice that opinion.

There were three trucks parked on one side of the otherwise empty lot. Two were late models, one red with lots of silver, one white. The other, a light gray, looked a good bit older. Cheney glanced back at him and then at the trucks and walked to the gray. Jonah smiled faintly as he unlocked the doors of the red.

Cheney spun on her heels and slid into the passenger's seat. "Everyone will see us coming from a mile away."

"They'll see us leaving first. We switch again in Taos."

She gave him a startled look. "You think we're being followed? Already?"

"No." He started the engine, then the AC. "Jade said it was just a precaution."

"Jade sounds bored," Cheney retorted.

"Likely, that too." He didn't look at her as he pulled forward on to the road. "Start talking."

For a moment, she didn't say anything. "About what?"

"About why you broke every single rule in the playbook." He glanced over at her stubborn silence. She was staring out the window on her side. Her jaw was clenched tight, and he decided to give her a minute or two before pressing for an answer.

When that answer came, it held more than a hint of anger. "This is my fight."

"How long have you known you were a Bellamy?"

Brows raised, she turned to face him. Yeah, it was a trick question considering he was the person who'd told her.

"Ten years," he answered himself, keeping his gaze on the road, "and in those ten years you haven't learned anything about this family?"

"Who would you like me to sacrifice?" She fired the question at him, still angry, but he heard the slight crack in her voice.

"Which of us do you think can't take care of themselves?" he fired right back.

Several miles ticked by in silence. "These guys aren't just murderers and thieves, Jonah. They aren't just thugs and gang-bangers. They're all that and more."

"And it's time we stopped them." He'd wanted to all those years ago, but sixteen-year-old Cheney had been the priority, getting her out, keeping her safe.

"I won't go home, Jonah."

"I said we, Cheney. I meant it. You and me." And whoever else they needed to bring in if things went south.

"You promise?"

He didn't hesitate. "I promise ... and I need the same from you."

At her silence, he glanced her way. Her gaze was on his face, and whatever she saw must have reassured her. She nodded, and Jonah let his shoulders relax a little. He didn't kid himself. This wouldn't be easy, and it would be doubly hard having Cheney beside him, at risk every step of the way, but the last thing he needed was for her to strike out on her own for lack of trust in him. She wasn't that teen-aged kid anymore. She was a skilled professional and a crack shot. She could more than handle herself, protect herself, and others, in a normal shitshow. But he had a feeling they were headed into something that was anything but normal.

* * *

"I read the file Frank gave you." He paused before adding, "On Quinn."

She didn't answer. She knew which file, and she knew he'd read it, had known before he sat down beside her on that bus.

"Cheney."

She sighed. "I figured that much since you were in my apartment."

Jonah didn't ask how she knew. It didn't matter anyway. He hadn't made any attempt to hide that he was there.

"So, what was your plan?"

"Infiltrate. Divide and conquer."

He waited, but that was all she had. Subterfuge wasn't

her strongest point.

"Not a bad strategy," he admitted.

"But?"

"It cuts us off from our resources."

She opened her mouth to argue that her plan hadn't included an 'us' and then closed it again. Nothing she did at this point would be enough for her to shake Jonah. So, use that, she told herself.

"Not if one of us is on the inside, one on the outside."

"That isn't going to happen. We stay together." She knew he waited for an argument but, when he glanced her way, she kept her gaze fixed on the mountain peaks that seemed to rise and fall in the distance with each passing mile.

Jonah glanced at the road then back at her to ask, "Did you dig that hat out of a dumpster?"

Her lips quirked in a half smile. "I washed it before I put it on."

"Thank God," but then he took a closer look and the amusement faded from his expression. "Pull it off."

"Why?" She knew why.

His silence had her lifting her hand and tugging the cap free. "It's called camel brown." She'd picked the hair color least likely to draw interested glances. Even the attractive model on the side of the box hadn't been able to make it look good.

"Well, it's brown, but I've got another adjective more apt than camel."

She bit back a smile. She felt sure she knew the word that came to his mind, so didn't bother to ask.

"Will it wash out?"

"Yeah." Just not quickly. She'd tucked a spare bottle into her bag just in case things took longer than she'd planned.

"Good."

She gave him a look, but his gaze stayed on the road as he asked, "Do you remember the day I took you to the family headquarters?"

She nodded, even though he wasn't looking at her. "Of course." She'd never forget. She'd been terrified.

* * *

Cheney tilted her head, staring up at the building in front of them. She felt dwarfed. And intimidated. She wouldn't admit it to the man beside her, but she never lied to herself. "This is it?" The urge to run hit her. Hard. But she'd seen enough of him by now to know he'd give chase. And he wouldn't give up. He'd already proven that.

"This is it."

She fought a sense of dread as they walked up to the security guard. She'd just showered but felt as grubby as the day Jonah found her. Even with all of the feelings boiling up inside her, she had too much pride not to put her shoulders back and lift her chin.

"Mike, this is Cheney. She's family."

Family. The idea petrified her. She didn't know any of them. She barely knew Jonah.

The guard nodded, giving her the same friendly, yet deferential smile he'd given Jonah.

The elevator that carried them up was smooth and silent. She felt Jonah watching her. He did that a lot.

Her boot heels clicked softly on the wide, stone floor of the hallway. The floor was so pretty she wanted to reach her hand down and touch it, but she didn't want to look dumb. Not in front of Jonah. On one side, most of the doors were closed. On the other, they stood open to offices where people talked and laughed. Her shoulders tensed with every curious glance toward the hallway as they walked past. On both sides, between doorways, hung portraits of varying sizes, mostly really big, none really small. The subjects portrayed seemed to watch her far more openly than the occupants of the offices.

Glancing up at one, she stopped in her tracks and her breath caught in her throat. Jonah smiled. "Maria Cordova Bellamy. Your many times great-grandmother."

The woman stared down at her with a half-smile and with eyes shaped like Cheney's own and almost as green. Even the shape of her face was the same. Cheney had noticed a redhead or two amongst the other portraits of mostly brunettes, but Maria's hair appeared to have been a summery mix of blonde and brown streaks. Cheney was mesmerized by the portrait, but Jonah touched her arm lightly, and her nerves jumped then settled. His family waited for them. Cheney felt certain that meeting couldn't go well, but there would never be a better time to know what lay ahead of her. Silently, she reminded herself that striking out on her own was always an option. Jonah would only drag her back so many times before he gave up on her.

Armed with that certainty, she could give this a try. She'd promised that much in a weak and grateful moment. She'd give it that much.

* * *

She felt Jonah's glance, knew he'd followed her thoughts where he'd intended them to lead her. "Watch the road." It was both a reminder and her defense against the look he directed her way.

He shifted his attention back to the pavement undulating in the heat but she felt him thinking. She knew why he'd asked her about that day. He knew her better than anyone. He always had. She'd seen the resemblance between herself and the woman she'd later learned was a strong and powerful matriarch. Her forebear. Jonah was reminding her of that, reminding her that not just Jonah, but those who'd sent him and those who'd come before them, had brought her home ... home to her family. Reminding her she wasn't in this—whatever this was—alone. He had her back as did dozens more back in Albuquerque.

What Jonah could never do, though, was give her the confidence of someone who had been brought up knowing they were a part of that dynasty. Cheney never felt, could never feel, that anything she did would ever make her completely one of them. She was grateful, so very grateful, for their generosity. She'd never take any of what she'd been given—a home, a job, a life—for granted. She'd also never stop wondering if one day she wouldn't be enough, and it would all be over.

* * *

Their stop in Taos was brief. The next truck that had been left for them was the ugliest beige she'd ever seen, and she cut Jonah a look, but all he did was shrug. She leaned in to look with him when he lifted the hood. The engine was powerful, and it was spotless. Jade was good, and she was thorough.

They tossed their duffels onto the narrow jump seat in the back and climbed into the front. Jonah started the motor, gunned it a little, and glanced at Cheney with a grin. She rolled her eyes and fought a grin of her own. Boys would always be boys. That engine had all the horsepower they might need and then some. It was still ugly, but ugly had its advantages. Like the dye on her hair.

They were near the state line when Jonah answered the call from Jade. Cheney recognized the voice, had been introduced to her early on, been with her in many meetings, and thought they might have been friends if life had been different. Not that they were enemies, but Cheney didn't make friends easily. She'd never learned to relate to normal people. Jade seemed very normal. Cheney envied her that.

"Where are you?"

"About to cross into Colorado." Cheney knew Jonah had heard the same tension that she had when he added, "Why?"

But all Jade said was, "Pull over and take me off speaker."

Cheney's heart sank as Jonah pulled to the shoulder. She forced herself to breathe evenly, to show no stress, but she felt certain her job was on the line. And that job ... this family were all she had. All she wanted.

As still as she sat, as hard as she tried, she could only hear Jonah's side of the conversation that ensued. And his side was all questions and silent listening. The last thing he said was, "I'll call back in ten minutes." He glanced toward Cheney, expression indecipherable. "Or less."

He broke the connection but didn't pull back onto the highway. Instead, he took a deep breath and met her gaze. "Who's Lina?"

She wanted to make a smartass comment, but at the look in his eyes, the comment died unspoken, and her blood chilled. She had to try twice before she could get any words past her stiff lips. "Someone who loves me."

"What haven't you told me?"

She didn't answer his question, just shook her head. She couldn't speak past the cold knot of dread that threatened to choke her.

With a quiet release of his breath, Jonah put the truck in drive then took the next exit to turn back toward

Albuquerque. Silent beside him, Cheney said nothing at all, but her heart was already shattering in her chest.

Chapter Five

The hospital was small, private. A half dozen or so police cars were scattered around the nearly empty parking lot. Two were pulled near the main entrance, facing outward. All of them had lights flashing in the dusky light, but their sirens were silent.

Jonah left the truck running and stepped out to walk around to the passenger side. Cheney hadn't spoken, had barely moved since he'd turned the rental around and headed back. He opened the door, and she looked at him with bleak eyes before she took the hand he held out to her and stepped down.

He nodded at the woman who emerged from his own truck, walked past him, and climbed into the driver's side of the rental. The rental would be returned. He and

Cheney would make other travel arrangements. Whatever had happened, their mission still lay before them. Cheney's mission was his, more so now than ever. His heart felt heavy for what she faced in the moments ahead.

Cheney tried to pull her hand from his as they walked toward the entrance, but he held tight. She was going to need him every bit as much as she would resent the fact later. So be it.

An older man in uniform, a hospital security emblem on his cap, fell into step beside them as they entered, then moved up to lead the way, pressing the elevator button, selecting the floor, then gesturing them toward the hallway beyond the re-opening door where another man waited.

Cheney had yet to speak, and Jonah respected her need for silence. He already knew what awaited them. Suspected she did as well. But she hadn't asked, and he'd respected that, too.

There was a guard on either side of the closed door. They each gave Jonah a nod, which he returned. One opened the door, and Jonah ushered Cheney inside where the physician waited.

"This is Ms. Navarro's niece."

There were no pleasantries. The doctor's eyes were kind but sad. "Next of kin?"

For a moment, Cheney seemed not to even breathe, then she nodded. "To my knowledge, the last of kin." She hesitated. "She's ... gone?"

"I'm sorry, truly sorry, yes, but to remove life support..."

Cheney's hand trembled in Jonah's.

"If you'd give us a moment," he said.

The physician nodded and left the room, murmuring. "I'll be just outside."

Cheney stepped closer to the hospital bed, pulled her hand from Jonah's, and placed it on the woman's face which looked peaceful. Jonah was grateful for small blessings, grateful that Cheney was spared the bruises and broken bones beneath the bedsheets, the shattered skull he'd been told lay under the covering of clean bandages that looked more like a hairdresser's wrap than medical dressings.

Cheney took the limp hand that lay upon the sheet, then leaned to press her lips to the woman's brow. "I'm sorry, Tia, so sorry." Her voice cracked. "This is my fault, because of me."

Jonah waited until she finally straightened with a shudder. When she did, he turned her to face him. "Not because of you, Cheney. Because of the evil that came to her shop, into her home. And this is one evil we'll end."

"Not we, Jonah." She took a deep breath and squared her shoulders. "This is my fight. I don't know why they came, after all this time, but they wouldn't have come here, done this, if they weren't looking for me."

"You're family, Cheney. You know what that means by now. No one's going to let you do this on your own. We'll take them down, but we'll do it together."

She lifted a devastated gaze to his. "Swear." It wasn't a plea. It was a demand, pure and simple.

"I swear." And that was a vow he'd keep, just as he'd hold her to the one she'd made not to shut him out of her search for Quinn and his family.

Before he requested the doctor to return, Jonah asked, "Do you want to wait here while…"

Cheney shook her head before he could finish. "Lina's already gone. We have work to do. I'm going to find and kill the bastard who laid hands on her." There was a quiet savagery in her voice.

Jonah didn't answer, but, if it could happen without harm to Cheney, he'd be glad to see her get that chance.

At the nurse's summons, the doctor stepped back into the room, but Jonah drew him aside until Cheney reluctantly released the hand of the woman who had loved her. And died for her.

Cheney didn't speak again until they were in the truck. "Take me to Old Town."

* * *

The road in front of Lina's shop was cordoned off. Police cars, mostly unmarked but always recognizable, lined the sidewalk. The night was so quiet that Cheney could hear the sound of her bootheels on the sidewalk. Too quiet.

Jonah guided her toward a plainclothes officer at the front door talking on a cell phone and pacing. As soon as he saw Jonah, the pacing stopped and the phone connection was ended. "Jonah." They shook hands, then he turned her attention to Cheney as Jonah introduced them.

"I'm sorry for your loss. Your aunt was respected and loved in Old Town."

"Thank you, Officer Moran." She took a deep breath. "What can you tell us?"

"Not much at this point. The place has been dusted for fingerprints, and we'll comb through whatever we find for matches but," he shook his head, "with the number of people who come in and out of these shops every day." He rubbed the back of his neck.

"Any thoughts?" Jonah pressed. "Any clues?"

"Maybe." He snapped his fingers at a younger man hovering in the background. "Where's that sleeve, Gable?"

Gable looked blank for a minute, then walked inside and returned with a plastic sleeve. Inside the clear plastic was an envelope.

Moran held it for a moment and looked from Jonah who'd asked the question, then to Cheney. "First thoughts ... this wasn't a simple robbery. The place was trashed and ... well ..."

Cheney knew what he wasn't saying. Her aunt could have simply been pushed aside or knocked unconscious, goods plundered, anything of value taken. That wasn't how it happened.

"Merchandise was ruined, not stolen. The cashbox wasn't touched ... and this was propped against it."

He handed the packet to Cheney who turned it over so that her aunt's neat handwriting was visible. It was addressed to Cheney in care of the Flannerys. The address was the main warehouse. Cheney had read it many times, always tucking it away in the desk that was reserved for Cheney and her homeschool lessons.

"She sent it for my sixteenth birthday," Cheney said numbly.

"To California?" Moran's look sharpened with that information. "Did you bring it with you to New Mexico?"

Cheney opened her mouth to speak, then just shook her head.

"No," Jonah answered. "She didn't."

She'd never returned to the warehouse or any of the Flannery homes. Everything she'd known ... everything she'd owned ... had remained in California, including this card.

* * *

The first faces she saw as she entered her aunt's shop were those of two of her co-workers, Angel Whittaker and Seth Reynolds. Neither spoke. Their eyes said it all, the sorrow, the anger, the need for violence, because they knew nothing they did could make this right and it hurt that they couldn't.

"Hey, guys," she said, surprised she could find her voice with her throat so tight and aching.

"Damn it," Angel said, brushing at the tears brimming in eyes the deep purple of a stormy, summer sky.

"Hey, kid," Seth said, although Cheney knew he wasn't all that much older than her.

She could feel them watching, feel their heartache for her loss as she walked slowly through the shop. Brightly colored shawls and scarves in tangles on the floor. Hand crafted leather bags slashed. Earrings both imported and from local Natives crushed beneath hard heels. The violence with which they'd destroyed Lina's shop was the violence with which they'd touched her. They'd hurt her, they'd meant to hurt her. And Cheney would hurt them.

When she turned back, her glance went to Jonah. He was half-turned, but she could tell his attention was in the exact place hers fell ... on the cashbox still under the counter. Untouched.

Jonah turned to meet her gaze. They both knew. This wasn't the work of a thief or an assassin. These were thugs, angry because they came looking for something—no ... for someone—they didn't find. Lina had paid the price. Cheney had been so careful, so very careful to keep her life separate from Lina's. But not careful enough. And she didn't kid herself. Whoever had sent them wasn't done. She'd be ready. Nor did she plan to wait for them to come to her.

A faint sound had her looking up sharply, then relaxing at the soft patter of rain on the roof.

She steadied her voice as she said aloud, "Who found her?"

An older, uniformed officer stepped from the rear of the shop, clipboard in her hand. "I did. I'm Officer Fallon. Sandra Fallon."

Her face was composed, but her eyes were sad. Pale hair was skimmed back from her face and knotted in a bun at the base of her neck. She wore no makeup and was the more attractive for the fact. Cheney didn't know her by name but she recognized her. She'd seen her here, with Lina.

"You were friends with her."

"Many years. We had coffee together every afternoon. I'd bring the cinnamon rolls for her sweet tooth, and she would make the coffee, always strong enough to keep me alert through the end of my shift." Her eyes filled. "I'm so sorry for your loss."

Cheney felt the stab of that loss again, and her heart hurt for both of them. "And I'm sorry for yours. Was she ... did she say anything?"

"I'm sorry, no. I was with her until the ambulance arrived. She never regained consciousness." She looked away for a moment. "I held her hand, but ... I'm not sure she knew."

Fighting the lump in her throat, Cheney touched the other woman's arm. "I'm sure. I'm sure she knew you were here for her."

She sensed when Jonah moved close behind her. It was time to go. There was nothing more she could do for Lina here. Vengeance would come, but not here.

"Officer Fallon—Sandra—I'd like for any merchandise,

anything salvageable, to be given to the neighboring shop owners. I'll sign whatever ..." her voice trailed as she realized she had other places to be, not more important than Lina but more urgent. Quinn.

"I'll call Jade," Jonah told her quietly, then looked at the police officer. "A family member will be in touch to take care of legalities and make sure Ms. Navarro's personal effects are secured for Cheney, if you'll help with the logistics of the merchandise."

Officer Fallon nodded and then looked away, blinking tears from her eyes.

* * *

As they left the Plaza, Jonah accepted that he couldn't take Cheney back to her apartment, not without posting a couple of guards. His next thought was to admit that he wouldn't, even if he thought that would be enough, that she'd be safe. He knew taking her to his apartment risked complications. He had no way of knowing if Angie had removed all of her belongings. They'd never moved in together, but things had a way of migrating between serious couples. Regardless, the only real risk was his own discomfort, and perhaps Angie's if she returned for something, but it was a risk he'd have to take.

They didn't talk on the way downtown or when Jonah pulled into the lower level of her apartment building and parked near the elevator, but when Cheney reached to open the truck door, he put his hand on her arm and said, "Wait."

The elevator door slid open and two men stepped out. One walked to the back of the truck, the other came toward her door. Jonah opened the door on his side at the same time hers was opened from the outside.

When Jonah walked around to her side of the truck, he pretended not to notice the look she shot him.

* * *

Cheney did her best to quell the frustration that swept her, held her tongue until they were inside the elevator, the door closed, and the two men left standing guard downstairs. "I can take care of myself, Jonah."

"Probably better than anyone I know," he agreed calmly. "Just not tonight."

He had, she realized, left her with nothing to argue. She wasn't surprised to find two more men outside her door. She was surprised when Jonah walked in with her.

"Didn't they sweep the place before we got here?"

"Yes. You'll need to gather some clothes."

She stopped and turned to face him. "I'd rather stay here."

He matched her look for look. Quinn, then Lina. He didn't need to say anything. She whirled back around and tossed her cap to the counter.

"And shampoo. Lots of shampoo." He was staring at her hair.

She walked into her room without answering, dumped her duffle filled with boys' clothing and tossed some of her own things in haphazardly. When she walked out, she found Jonah in her bathroom, opening and closing drawers.

"What the hell, Jonah?"

"I'm trying to help. We're both tired and need something to eat. And drink." She had a feeling he wasn't talking about ice water or tea. "Where's your makeup and stuff?"

She stared at him. "When have you *ever* seen me in makeup?"

He stared back. "You don't wear makeup?"

She pushed him to one side and moved past without answering to grab her soap and lotion and shampoo. Tossing them into her duffle along with her toothpaste and brush, she walked back out.

* * *

Wherever Cheney had expected to be taken—a hotel, maybe, one secured by guards—it wasn't his high rise. At least as much of a high rise as the city could claim. It was at least level with the tops of surrounding buildings. She'd never been inside, had never expected to be, but she knew exactly where she was when he pulled into the parking garage, the gates sliding shut behind them. She also knew he spent holidays and plenty of weekends at the ranch and that he had a cabin in the mountains for weekend getaways with friends. And with his fiancée.

His fiancée. "This isn't a good idea," she said quietly when he cut the ignition.

"Got a better one?"

"Only a hundred."

He snorted. "Let's go."

He grabbed her bag as they climbed out. A movement caught her eye, and she glanced back as the security team resumed their places behind the iron gates.

The elevator was smooth, and it was silent, as was the entry space it opened onto. Cheney lifted a brow. "An entire floor?"

Jonah shrugged and gestured for her to step out. The space was unexpected. It wasn't the chill sophistication she might have anticipated. Instead, it was as inviting as a country home albeit a classy one. She followed him down the hall to a bedroom decorated in shades of coral. He placed her duffle just inside her door.

He paused there, facing her. "We have a meeting first thing in the morning."

"Meeting? With whom?"

"Jade, Colter ... my parents and anyone they choose to pull in."

She grimaced. "I'm sure your parents will be thrilled to see me again."

Jonah tilted his head quizzically, then smiled. "I suspect they will, at that."

Feeling confused and more than a little lost, she hunched her shoulders. "What's this meeting about?"

"Strategic planning."

"Is your father a good strategist?" Dumb question, she thought. Marcus Slade was good at everything that came his way.

"Dad? Not particularly, but my mom is the best. I'm not half bad, but she still has me beat." His lips quirked, and she was reminded just what his smile did to her insides. "Hungry?"

"Not particularly, but a glass of wine would be nice. Maybe a Chardonay, if you have it?"

"I'm sure I have something decent and wouldn't mind one myself."

She followed him back down the hall and regretted her suggestion as soon as he flipped on the kitchen light. He glanced at the counter, hesitated, then opened the wine chiller as if he hadn't seen the engagement ring, along with a key, placed carefully atop a folded note. She opened her mouth to speak but couldn't think of a damned thing to say.

Turning, he touched his finger to her chin, nudging as if to close her mouth. She did.

"Leave it, Cheney. This is on us—me and Angie—not you. It was coming, regardless."

She didn't believe that was true, but she took the glass of wine he handed her and fled, taking her demons with her.

* * *

Jonah turned off the overhead light took his own glass and sat in the dim glow of undercabinet lighting. He knew he was brooding over something he wouldn't go back and change even if he could, but he couldn't pretend he didn't have regrets. Not until he was certain that Cheney slept, did he open the note from Angie.

This hurts as much as I knew it would. It hurts mostly because I always half-expected it to happen but kept telling myself it wouldn't. And I'm mad as hell because I gave so much of myself, my time, my energy to this ... to us. I love you. I suspect I always will. Angie

Placing his half-empty wine glass on the counter, he went to his room where he dropped the ring into a dresser drawer before heading for the shower. He paused to open the closet door on his way. His shirts hung neatly on one side, pants on the other. Nothing of Angie's remained. He hadn't thought there would be. While he didn't feel the sharp knife of heartbreak, there was the sad ache of regret.

One day he hoped to tell Angie that, to make sure she knew his feelings had been real. Real, but not enough. For now, his focus had to be Cheney, who—since the day he'd found her—had haunted a quiet corner of his mind. Just as Angie had implied.

Sleep was a long time coming for many reasons and,

when he woke, it was to the smell of bacon burning and the sound of Cheney cursing under her breath. Ignoring both, he headed for the shower. He was way too smart to walk into that room until she had things, herself included, under control.

* * *

Cheney had awakened to dreams of the first day she'd followed Jonah into Bellamy headquarters, her first glimpse of her ancestress, her first meeting with Jonah's parents.

At the end of the long hall, Jonah touched her arm and gestured toward a set of double-doors. The doors were flung wide to a small sitting area with a bank of windows beyond. She was, she realized, on the top floor of the building. She also realized the building was tall but not sky-scraper tall as it had seemed from the sidewalk.

Jonah stayed a step behind her as she approached the older couple who'd stood up from the small sofa. "My parents," he said, "Marcus and Eden Slade."

Cheney put her hands behind her back. "I'm Cheney."

The woman noted her movement then lifted her gaze back to Cheney's. Jonah's mother neither opened her arms to embrace Cheney nor reached out a hand to shake hers. Nothing in her gaze reflected warmth enough to make Cheney think she might have done so otherwise.

"We're glad you're here," Eden said, then looked from Cheney to Jonah, "and grateful to you, son, for her rescue, even more grateful to have you both safely home."

Home. Cheney thought that an odd choice of words. Jonah had told her she would be educated and given an opportunity to work for the company or helped to find work elsewhere if that was what she chose. She'd thought long and hard before accepting but had finally nodded, knowing she would find a way to pay it all back. But this was not home to her.

"I'd have known you for a Bellamy," Marcus said, after an appraising look at her features. "Welcome home." And there it was, that word again. They were so ... accepting of her presence. She'd come to trust Jonah, but she didn't trust much else. His father's gaze, at least, seemed more welcoming. His mother's remained cool and watchful.

The other person in the room, a man about Jonah's age, stepped closer. "I'm Colter Bellamy. My parents are waiting impatiently to meet you as are the rest, but all that can wait. Jonah messaged that you'd both be hungry when you arrived so food first."

Completely overwhelmed, Cheney had never felt less hungry, but a table had been laid in an adjoining room and a servant stood quietly, waiting to serve.

As they were seated and Cheney unfolded her napkin to place it in her lap. She looked up to find Eden watching her.

"You have the look of her. Of Maria."

Cheney hadn't a clue how to answer. She didn't want to look like a long dead Bellamy. She didn't want to be here. She wanted to go home, but there was nothing and no one to go home to. She lifted her chin as Eden's gaze searched hers, looking for all of the secrets that lay buried. She wouldn't find them. No one would.

In the silence that followed, Marcus asked, "What do you want to do with your life now?" As if she really had a choice.

She thought of Jonah, the trouble he'd gone to find her, the risks he'd taken to save her. And she thought of where she'd come from, where she'd been. All she could think to say was, "Stop the bad guys."

And this time it was Marcus who did no more than nod. As if everything were that simple.

* * *

And, in the end, much of it turned out to be. Cheney had chosen homeschool over traditional school plus job training with Welles Enterprises, all while attending college. College would have been easier had it been her only focus, but she loved every moment of rotation through the various arms of the company. Except the ranch. Cheney and ranch work did not get along, but she'd done her stint there without uttering a single complaint.

In the decade since that first meeting, Marcus and Eden had divorced. Their breakup had supposedly been fiery, tumultuous, and very, very bitter but no one seemed to know quite what caused the split. Or the ones who did weren't talking. Since then, Cheney had attended meetings with both of them present and had never seen a sign of the reputed drama except in Eden's eyes when she looked at her ex-husband.

His parents had never once made her feel unwelcome, but she couldn't imagine they'd been impressed by a sixteen-year-old with raggedly cut hair and a sketchy past.

And, just after midday, when she and Jonah walked into the conference room where his parents waited with Jade, it was her hair that once again drew the attention.

Chapter Six

Jade stood first, wincing at the sight of Cheney. "Good God."

Cheney wasn't that self-conscious teenager anymore, and she lifted one brow.

"Sorry. I'm sorry," Jade looked instantly contrite as she came close and wrapped Cheney in a hug. She didn't even look offended at Cheney's stiff response when she stepped back to study her. It was no secret that Cheney didn't care to be greeted with a hug. "I actually think the boy-cut is cute on you but not the mud brown." Despite the light comment, Jade's eyes held a wealth of sadness. "We'll find whoever hurt your aunt. I promise."

For Cheney, it wasn't a question of who. The question was why. Or, at least, why *now*.

Marcus had his cell phone to his ear and paced back and forth across the room as he talked in low tones. As she always did, Cheney saw Jonah in his father's straight back and lithe movements. When he slipped his phone back into his pocket, he said to no one in particular, "Colter's caught in a traffic jam, but he'll be here in a few."

Eden's gaze went straight to Cheney and held until Jade moved away and Cheney could give Jonah's mother her full attention. "We'll put together a plan, a solid one. You're not to take off on your own." When Cheney said nothing, she persisted. "I know you're thinking it."

"She's already given her word," Jonah interjected.

Eden's gaze pinned Cheney as she answered her son. "She may have, but it's still in her mind."

Cheney lifted her chin. "No one else needs to take the kind of risk that comes with these people. Lina's dead," she said bluntly. "They battered and broke her. Is that what you want for Jonah?"

And that was unjust, she knew, but Eden didn't so much as flinch. Instead, she studied Cheney for a long moment, as if reading her thoughts, and Cheney thought maybe she was.

"I want my son to be safe. If you run, he'll follow, and he'll be more at risk chasing you than if he's *with* you, guarding your back while you guard his." Her mouth quirked in a smile she almost allowed to surface. "As I know you can and would ... as I know you will."

Cheney hated that the other woman was right. Nothing anyone said would stop Jonah trailing her. She didn't understand all the reasons that he would, she just knew it was so.

"I won't run," she said when Eden refused to look away.

Eden didn't ask for a promise. She dipped her chin in acknowledgement or appreciation or, perhaps, a little of both. "Thank you."

* * *

Colter arrived moments ahead of the food delivery service, a casual blend of sandwiches, wraps, and salads. Cheney didn't feel particularly hungry but she very much wanted a glass of that wine chilling in a bucket of ice so she filled a plate when the others did, took a glass that was poured for her, then chose a seat some distance from the sofa and grouping of armchairs around the low table that centered them.

Facing her accusers was the thought that popped into her head, although she knew it wasn't true. Never once had they judged or been critical, but she'd never felt a part of this family. She couldn't relate to that casual camaraderie they shared with such ease.

She didn't, for example, feel comfortable enough to ask them to just get on with the plan so that she could get on the road. Jade could have pulled that off with her easy, breezy style—meant it but left everyone laughing.

Partly, Cheney knew, it was because this didn't just involve her. It would be her and Jonah. Nothing easy, breezy about that. And it would do no good to tell anyone in this room that she could travel faster and work better alone. Even if they believed that, they wouldn't go for it. That, she'd learned, was also what *family* meant. This family, anyway.

Jade began the work part of the gathering, setting up her computer and lowering a screen from a sidewall with the touch of a button. "We're starting with the theory that this was a random robbery…"

Cheney opened her mouth to protest but closed it as Jade finished her sentence.

"…and debunking it as we go. These are stills captured from various storefront security cameras. Pay attention to height, shoulder width, and jawline. And footwear."

A photo with the date in small letters appeared on the screen. Three men passed in front of Lina's shop. Their stride was unhurried. None of them glanced toward the storefront but seemed intent upon their conversation. All three wore their hair in tight buns low on the back of their necks.

Cheney quickly cataloged the images. Height not above—maybe even slightly less than—average, eyes dark, hair dark, body mass indeterminate due to the relaxed cut of faded jeans and hoodies. What stood out to her were the familiar square lines of their jaws, the almost elegant slope of their noses.

The next several shots, different dates and times, showed them in varying styles. Hair left loose with tight-fit jeans and muscle shirts, pulled into ponytails with business suits, and stuffed under less-than-clean caps with the hodgepodge clothing of the homeless. Sometimes they wore sunshades, sometimes not. Sometimes, they walked apart from each other, mixed with a crowd around them, but Cheney picked them out of that crowd before Jade pointed them out. In some, it was just the three of them again, moving as a team.

The only thing that did not change was a pair of sandals that one of them wore consistently.

"Why the hell didn't he change footgear?" Colter wondered aloud. "Why chance it?"

Jade shrugged. "If you look closely, you'll see the small

toe on the left foot was broken at one time and healed badly. Those sandals, that brand, was ultra pricey originally and just as pricey to replace, now. They're well-worn and undoubtedly comfortable. And who pays attention to shoes?"

You, Cheney thought silently, impressed because the disguises had been good. Their behavior had been normal. Even she might not have noticed the sandals had Jade not mentioned footwear up front.

The last few photos came from cameras inside the businesses that were closest to Lina's. The lenses had captured several singles of each of the three, sometimes appearing interested in the merchandise, sometimes at the windows or entryway watching passersby. The features were blurred but, for Cheney, the lines of the faces were unmistakable. As were the eyes when not covered by sunglasses.

"The shots were sequential, but the dates aren't close together."

Jade nodded at Marcus' comment. "No, they watched the shop for well over two weeks."

"When was the first date they were seen in Old Town?" Eden asked. "I should have paid attention."

But Cheney had. It was three days after Quinn Flannery and his family were declared missing.

When Jade answered Eden's question, it was Jonah who voiced Cheney's thoughts. "Just enough time to lay low for a day or two after and make their way here."

She felt his gaze on her, and the others turned toward her as well. She shifted to meet those looks. *His* look. "Who are they?"

"The sons of Raul Aguilar." Older, harder.

"What are they looking for?" Marcus asked.

"Me," Cheney said honestly.

"Why?"

Inwardly, Cheney felt gutted as memories of Kell's murder swamped her. Outwardly, she feigned indifference. "Maybe because I'm the one that got away." This time her answer was something less than honest and, judging by the look in Jonah's eyes, he knew it.

"Someone, probably multiple someones, had to have worked all night to pull these photos together," Marcus said, looking at Jade who nodded. "Give them my thanks and whatever else you think would be appreciated."

"My assistant is putting some weekend packages together. Most of the team are already dreaming of city lights or white sandy beaches," Jade said, then shifted her gaze to Jonah's mother who stood and began slowly pacing along the edge of the room.

After a moment, Eden looked straight at Jonah. "We'll have to work just as fast to pull a plan together."

Cheney noticed he was smart enough not to take that look as an invitation to take over. All he said was, "Or faster."

Eden's gaze went to Cheney. "Who do they work for?"

"Themselves." Cheney's voice was quiet and cool. She kept her gaze on Eden as steady as her voice.

"So, they're the traffickers who held you." It wasn't a question. "And you think they've been looking for you for ten years." Still no question. When it came, it was pointed but not accusing. "Do you think they look for every young girl who manages to escape them? Because I doubt you were the first. At least I hope you weren't."

Cheney sent Jonah a glance, then refocused on his mother. "No," she said quietly, "but I'm the one who killed their father."

Eden shot Jonah a look, but Cheney could feel his glare locked on her. He was more than angry. His struggle for control was an almost physical presence in the room.

"I don't think this is something that should have been kept quiet, son."

Jonah opened his mouth to speak, but Cheney beat him to it. "He didn't know. I didn't tell him."

It was Colter who broke the silence that blanketed the room. "Well. Hell."

Jade leaned back in her seat. "This gives a new perspective. Definitely a shift in tactics from what I was thinking."

"There's no need for tactics," Cheney said quietly. "I'll leave as soon as we're done, and that will end this for all of you. They won't bother anyone here as long as I'm not, and I'll make sure they know."

"The hell you will," Jonah growled.

"Jonah's right," Marcus spoke firmly. "You're family. We take care of our own."

Jonah stood. "Guys, I need a little time with Cheney."

"You can use my office, son," Marcus answered. "We'll be here when you get back."

"Jonah?" Eden's tone wasn't harsh, but it was firm. "Be brief. We have work to do."

Cheney didn't bother to object. When Jonah turned to look at her, she stood and followed him from the room.

Marcus' office was at the end of the hall. Jonah held the door for her and closed it behind them. "Sit wherever."

Marcus' office felt like him, she thought. Expansive windows, man-sized furniture, lots of leather and wood. No sleek sophistication. Only strength. Like Jonah.

Ignoring the sofa, she crossed to the small table with four comfortable chairs. She took one that placed her back to the wall. Jonah sat opposite her and the room fell into total silence for several long moments.

"Talk," he said finally.

She lifted her gaze from her hands to his face. His tone wasn't what she'd expected. The anger she'd seen in his eyes—if she really had—was gone. He almost sounded defeated, and that was an emotion she'd never seen or heard in him, in any of them.

Her heart cracked a little deeper. It seemed to do that with every encounter they had. She wanted to say she was sorry, because she truly was, but the words wouldn't matter. Words never did.

"You know most of it," she said finally.

"Then tell me what I don't know."

She forced her shoulders to relax. She had a feeling Jonah knew much of what she was about to say, but it was where she needed to begin. "Raul Aguilar started out as a small-time smuggler, getting people across the border, both into and out of the States. Not like what's happening now. These were people with money, usually South American or Asian, many of them arriving through, but not necessarily from, Mexico. Some escaping persecution for religious or political beliefs or a death threat simply because they had money or property some third world leader desired. Others were established criminals elsewhere who wanted new identities in America. Some were established criminals here who wanted new identities elsewhere. At first, only one or two a year, but he had good contacts who were skilled at making them vanish into new lives once they crossed. His reputation grew and so did his business."

"I take it the Flannerys were those good contacts on this side."

"There were others, I think, maybe a lot of others.

Aguilar played his end close to the vest. As best as I could tell, he and his sons controlled everything. He told no one more than they needed to know for whatever transaction was in process."

"So, the Flannery warehouse business, like the ones your father managed, was just a front."

She frowned, then shook her head. "No. The warehouses were just what they were supposed to be. And they were profitable. Besides … my dad … he wouldn't have."

Jonah leaned back in his chair and stared her down. "Not even to keep you from starving?"

She wouldn't lie and honestly didn't know what her father would have done to keep her safe. "The warehouses he managed stored heavy equipment for contractors. I saw the machinery moved in and out as jobs opened and shut down. The business was real."

But they both knew the rigs that hauled the equipment in and out could have hauled other things as well, human things. She thought Jonah would call her on that but all he said was, "What brought you to Aguilar's attention? Made him decide he'd have you? That's what happened, wasn't it?"

Jonah's jaw was clenched, and there was murder in his eyes. She met that look without flinching. "That's what happened," she said quietly.

Chapter Seven

The man strode into the Flannery warehouse as if he were walking into his castle, as if he already owned it. Cheney didn't know him, had never seen him. High cheek-boned and swarthy complexion. Hispanic, she thought. Arrogant, she was certain. And his eyes promised he was just as cruel.

The two men who flanked him had the same conceit about them, the same expensive dark suits, the same flat look to their eyes, and the same hard angle of jawline.

These were not the usual type men she saw in the warehouse. She felt it and knew that her father did as well when he walked to the end the counter and stepped from behind it but went no further than the end where his shotgun leaned against a shelf. He glanced back at Cheney as he pulled it close and motioned toward the back room with his chin. She slipped quietly from her stool, taking the scissors from the countertop in a surreptitious movement. She left the door partway open but stood to one side, just out of their sight. It was plain her father didn't care for the looks of the men and she didn't either. She also didn't like her father being alone in the cavernous warehouse with them. But for her to be there, would have been a distraction for him.

"I am Aguilar."

She wished she could see her father's face, wanted to be by his side but she didn't dare move, didn't dare distract him. Say something, she pleaded silently, but her father wasn't one to play another man's game, and he waited in silence.

"Where's Flannery?"

"Which one?"

"The oldest. The owner."

"They're all partners to my knowledge, and I don't know which of them is the oldest." Her father's voice was quiet, but she heard the edge of warning in it. Don't, Daddy, she thought, her heart racing. Just tell them anything they want to know, even if it's a lie, so they'll go away.

"Smart one, aren't you?"

"Smart enough."

"You like to play with knives?" Aguilar taunted.

Cheney heard what sounded like the slap of a blade against a palm and her stomach roiled.

"Do you like to play with bullets?" her father countered with a blast of his gun, the bullet making a ringing sound when it hit the metal of the warehouse roof.

Aguilar's only answer was a jeering snicker and a thud, followed by a sharp grunt of pain. "Play with that, old man."

The gun fired again, then the stock hit the floor with a thud.

"Nooo," Cheney moaned at the sound of laughter from the men.

Tears sliding down her cheeks, heart pounding, she gripped the scissors at her side as a single pair of footsteps closed the distance between her and the men outside. Aguilar pushed the door open slowly and grinned at her. "You're a pretty little girl. I'll turn you into a pretty little whore."

Fear for her father paralyzed her as Aguilar kept walking toward her. She took a deep breath to steady herself. When he was close enough, she plunged the closed blades of the scissors into his stomach just below his waistline, then twisted hard as her father told her she should do with a knife. Aguilar's eyes widened and he grunted, as he clutched the end of the scissors. The flow of his blood spread a scarlet stain across the front of his pale blue dress shirt.

She knew his sons would kill her, but at least she'd killed him.

From beyond the small room, Kell Flannery's voice, hard with rage, echoed through the warehouse. "Don't either of you move. Not an inch. Cheney? Cheney answer me!"

"I'm here." Her voice was no more than a broken whisper. "I'm here."

* * *

"Your father was murdered. Unprovoked and in cold blood. That's not exactly how Kell told it." Jonah's stare was steady and hard. "And you never told me any different."

"You never asked."

"Damn it, Cheney."

She just looked at him, her heart still raw with the remembering, even after all these years. Sometimes in the night, she would see her father's body on the floor, surrounded by his blood. Sometimes in the night, she would see the hatred on Raul Aguilar's face as his sons helped him from the room. She had no doubt he'd cursed her, no doubt that she *was* cursed.

Jonah sighed. "So, Aguilar lived?"

"No. At least not very long. The blade of the scissors went into his intestines. He got sepsis in the hospital. Kell told me it was a slow way to die, an ugly way. I'm glad."

But his sons had vowed revenge, and Kell said she couldn't stay so he'd begun looking for the only family she had, the family her father had told Kell she had. The family she'd never known existed. The day after they buried her father, he'd taken her to a man who duplicated the tattoo that was on his arm, as well as those of his brothers, on her arm. It was the best and only protection he could offer her.

She'd stood in her room after and stared at the deep blue ink of the barbed wire that wrapped itself all the way around her arm above the elbow. The only difference between hers and the Flannery brothers was that theirs ended in arrow tips and hers ended in tiny leaves. Kell said it was a symbol that she was under their protection, close enough to fool anyone from a distance yet different enough that she could disassociate herself if that needed to happen. Kell's goal had been to keep her safe until someone came for her. Cheney hoped that wouldn't happen. The Flannerys were all she knew; all she had left of her father.

But Jonah *had* come and, ten years later, she still wasn't sure if that was a good thing or a bad thing.

* * *

When Cheney fell silent, Jonah kept a tight lid on the questions her revelations had stirred in his mind. Somewhere in his files, he still had a copy of the handwritten note, signed by Kell Flannery and addressed to Welles Enterprises. It had been hand-delivered by courier, then scanned and emailed to Jonah who'd been headed home from Montana following what proved to be a dead-end lead on another case. He'd read it sitting in the back booth of a truck stop, his second cup of coffee growing cold.

The information Flannery had provided was sparse and simply written but enough to have him phoning Jade with his change in travel plans. Cheney, sixteen years old and a Bellamy by blood, was now orphaned. Her father had been an innocent bystander killed in a turf war between rival gangs. Flannery would keep her as safe as he could for as long as he could but she needed family. Jonah had replied with three words. *On my way*.

Things he'd thought he knew were no longer adding up. He wanted answers, and he'd get them, but now was not that time. As if to prove his point, his mother tapped on the doorframe, drawing their attention.

"Jonah."

He got to his feet and Cheney did the same, but Eden stopped her at the door. "A moment?"

Jonah turned, ready to protest, "Mom…"

"It's fine, Jonah," Cheney said quietly. "This won't take long."

He looked from one to the other then gave in at the resolute gazes that met his. "Five minutes."

He walked back to the conference room, took his seat, and glanced around the table. He gave a slight shrug at the lifted brows then shared what he'd learned from Cheney.

Jade was first to break the silence that followed. "Well … that changes things."

Jonah watched as she disconnected her laptop from the wall projector and went to work on revising their plan.

Chapter Eight

Cheney watched as Eden came into the room and closed the door behind her. For a moment, the two women stood in silence, taking each other's measure. It was Cheney who spoke first.

"You don't want him going with me," she said, flatly. "I don't either. I'd stop him if I could."

Eden tilted her head, studying her. "I believe you. I also know you can't stop him. He's in love with you."

Cheney stared, dumbfounded. "You're wrong."

"I wish I were. Even he doesn't know it yet." Her lips curved faintly, not quite a smile, but close.

"They'll work things out. He and Angie. Once I'm out of the way."

Cheney wasn't surprised when Eden ignored her

comment and murmured instead, "You won't make life easy for him. You haven't since he first learned of your existence. That's not going to change."

Cheney fought the urge to drop her gaze. She'd be damned if she'd let herself look weak in front of a woman as strong as Eden Slade. "Life isn't *ever* easy."

"Not for any of us," Eden agreed, "but Slades only love once. They love fiercely and long ... but only once."

The statement, not anything she was expecting to hear, startled Cheney. "Did Marcus not love you?"

"Fair question," Eden murmured.

Cheney hadn't meant it to be fair, just honest. She hadn't meant it to be brutal either, but she supposed it had been.

Eden finally nodded. "He did. Marcus loved me with all of his heart. He still does. As I love him with all of mine. Sometimes love isn't enough. It should be ... but it isn't."

"So, what am I supposed to do with this wealth of knowledge?" Cheney asked with more than a touch of frustration.

Eden chuckled ruefully. "Damned if I know."

To Cheney's surprise Eden drew her in for a hug. "For now, be safe, and keep my son safe as he'll do for you. We'll figure the rest out later."

Eden turned to walk out but stopped at the door and looked back as Cheney hesitated. "Come on, then, let's see what Jade has cooked up in that wickedly clever brain of hers."

More confused than anything else, Cheney followed, slipping into the only seat remaining. Beside Jonah.

* * *

Jade held command of the room as she talked, beginning with an abbreviated summary of the death of Cheney's father before turning to a recap of Flannery Warehousing. There were several aerial maps on a drop-down projection screen. She pointed to two large buildings, separated by multiple city streets and marked with bold red X's. "Flannery Warehousing has been in operation for decades, starting small with these two warehouses that were initially on the outskirts of a town that has long since grown up around them. There are four additional warehouses further out of the city and a couple more right on the docks."

"Their client base?" Colter asked.

"Largest and oldest are two heavy equipment contractors. With the growth of the city, those clients moved from the two original buildings to the four located in less congested areas. Those warehouses also serve several commercial construction contractors."

"And the two downtown?"

"They serve a variety of businesses," Jade answered Jonah. "From clothing store surplus to old records storage for city hall and just about anything in between."

"Anything suspicious in their accounting?" The question came from Marcus.

No one questioned the ability of Jade's team to hack into their financials.

For the first time, Jade appeared hesitant. "Not that I've found ... I'm still sorting through."

Colter straightened in his chair. "But?"

"Not really. Not yet. Just a feeling."

But Cheney knew as well as the rest of them that Jade's *feelings*, however vague, rarely—if ever—turned out to be completely wrong. Nor was Cheney naïve enough to think that the Flannerys were above small illegalities if business warranted, but they weren't thieves and they helped far more people than the average citizen who made do-good contributions to big name charities. And, for her, none of the rest mattered.

"So, how do we get on the inside with the Aguilars?" At the moment, that was all Cheney cared about, getting in and finding Quinn and his family. If they were alive. If not, then all she would care about was taking out the last of the Aguilar band, to the final man.

Jade looked at Eden whose gaze held Cheney's as she shook her head. "You don't."

Cheney leaned back in her chair. Now wasn't a time or place to argue. Actually, there was never a time or place for argument. Not in Cheney's world. If she disagreed, she simply moved on and did what she knew to do.

The faintest smile curved Eden's mouth as if she knew Cheney's thoughts. And maybe she did. "You and Jonah are going to bring them to you."

Cheney let some of the tension out of her spine. Maybe, just maybe, Jonah's mother really did understand.

Jade looked across the table. "Colter, I sent you a packet of information earlier."

He nodded, staring at his screen. "I'm looking at it now." He got to his feet. "I think some of this will go smoother with phone calls than email. I'll be in my office if you need me."

"All I gave you was bare bones. How, when, where or whatever you think works. Just send me the final when you finish. Oh, and there are two police officers waiting outside. If you don't mind sending them in, we'll get things rolling here."

Colter rose and walked around to place a hand on Cheney's shoulder. She met his gaze, reading the reassurance mixed with a touch of wry humor. "Whatever you've got in mind to do, just don't. Give us a chance to do what we do best."

The knot in her throat tightened. Letting others control her plans and her fate didn't come easily. When she finally nodded, he smiled and murmured. "That's our girl." His tone, as much as the comment, reverberated through her. Yes, she'd accepted that she was a part of this family, that had been drilled into her time and again—mostly by Jonah—but the words rang different this time.

She set that thought aside for now and watched as Jonah walked with him to the door where they stood in brief conversation, followed by an even briefer but strong hand clasp.

They left the door open and moments later, two plainclothes officers walked in, stopping just inside the open door.

This time it was Jonah who took the lead, gesturing to the officers to take a seat and making introductions around the room. Meanwhile, Jade sat quietly jotting notes that Cheney suspected had nothing whatsoever to do with the discussion in progress.

Both of the officers turned their attention to Cheney but it was the younger, taller of the two who spoke to her. "You have the sympathy of our entire division. Your aunt was both well respected and sincerely liked."

Cheney nodded and murmured her appreciation. A simple thank you was all she could manage around the lump in her throat.

He turned his attention to Jonah. "Mr. Slade, I'll be honest with you. We've found very little to explain the attack on Lina Navarro. We've read through all of the statements and understand that Ms. Navarro's shop, like that of her neighbors, brought in enough to make a living but not much more. Nothing seemed to have been taken, not even what little cash was in the box." He glanced regretfully at Cheney before adding, "The attack was violent and destructive with no apparent motive."

"So, the case is closed?" Cheney asked.

He tugged at his collar. "No, ma'am, not closed. We'll be watching for links to anything else that might happen in the area."

But there wouldn't be, she knew. The Aguilars hadn't found the one thing they were looking for. They wouldn't stop searching, but neither would they waste their time terrorizing other shop owners or residents in their hunt for Cheney.

When they left, Jonah handed their written report to Jade who laid it to one side with a nod. Her gaze went straight to Cheney. "Are you okay?"

Cheney lifted her chin. "I will be." When the bastards were dead.

"Then let's get started."

The first screen Jade pulled up was a newspaper article. Cheney read it in silence, then read it again.

The article was a stark recounting of the murder of Lina Navarro and the disappearance of her niece, with a reward offered by an unnamed source for information leading to the arrest of the perpetrator. The wording was vague as to whether Cheney might be wanted for questioning or was thought to be endangered.

"So, am I supposed to be kidnapped, dead, or guilty?"

"Depends on who's asking that question." Jade lifted a brow. "The two detectives on the case won't ask. The Aguilars know it's none of the above so we hope they believe you're on the run or lying low."

"Which I won't," Cheney said flatly. "Either one."

"Far from it," Eden agreed with a smile.

"When was this released?" Marcus asked

"It hasn't been, yet. It will be in this evening's edition. Too soon and it would've looked like someone worked all night to make it happen," Jade added wryly.

Jade changed screens. Instead of a newspaper article, the print looked like that of a magazine. Jonah said as much by way of a question, and Cheney was absurdly pleased that he didn't seem to know much more than she did about what was happening so swiftly around them.

"It is," Jade said calmly in response to Jonah's query. "One of South America's better known online fashion magazines."

"What does a sneak-peak at an emerging super model have to do with our case?"

It was Jonah who asked the question, but it was Cheney whose eyes widened in horror when, instead of answering, Jade used the cursor to flip the page on the article. Cheney stared at the chiseled chin and high cheekbones in the photograph. But the eyes staring back from her face in the photograph were blue rather than green and her normal red-gold hair had more gold and bronze than red.

"Oh ... oh no, no, no ... we're so not doing this. It will never work."

"It will work," Eden said calmly. "Jade, this is brilliant."

"What's next?" Jonah asked as if this—whatever this was Jade proposed—were no big deal, and Cheney glared at him.

"Your inbox is full of info my team have been gathering." She cut him a sidelong look. "Along with a few playscripts I sent for you to consider once the two of you reach Argentina. Colter is currently playing security manager, making calls all across Europe, scoping out venues, and ensuring safety for Charlsey and her entourage as she makes her global debut. Meanwhile, Cheney and I will be focused on turning her into the next up and coming model."

"That will certainly fail," Cheney muttered

"I suspect she's hungry," Jade told Jonah, not bothering to refute Cheney's comment. "I'll order something delivered when we get to her new apartment."

"With alcohol," Cheney said, then scowled. "What new apartment?"

"Just temporary. You and I are going to work from there this afternoon and regroup here in the morning with an expanded team. I have a few more things to wrap up, and we'll go. If you'd rather head out now, I'll call a security detail to go with you."

"That's bull." Cheney stood. "I don't need security. I *am* security."

"I'll get her there safely," Jonah shot her a look and countered firmly. "The fewer people we involve, the fewer chances of a mishap."

"Don't forget the whiskey," Cheney glared at Jade.

* * *

Whiskey or not, Jonah didn't have much hope the afternoon would go any smoother than the morning. Cheney ignored him as they walked out of the conference room and down the hall.

They stepped into the elevator, and Jonah pressed the button for the parking garage.

"I need to go by my apartment."

"According to one of Jade's notes—you're included

on all of them so you can read when we get settled—your apartment has already been cleaned out and your belongings moved to the new place."

Cheney said an ugly word, uglier, she knew, than Jonah liked to hear from anyone. But she had to hand it to him, he ignored it with a patient expression while he continued with the information he'd been given.

"Your belongings have been relocated, but one of the staff is accepting flowers and condolences and meal deliveries as well as dealing with a horde of mourners in the entryway of your own apartment because you are currently *indisposed* and not accepting visitors."

"Indisposed? What the hell does that mean?"

"Whatever is interpreted by the visitor."

She gave him a sour look. "Lovely."

Jonah tried to hide his smile ... unsuccessfully. "You have a better idea?"

Cheney snorted but didn't bother to give him an answer. She doubted he expected one.

The apartment building, across town from hers, was one that had been available to her for years and was far more impressive than the more modest place she preferred. By the time she'd believed she earned it, she was content where she was and had never felt any need to upgrade. An apartment, like a bed, was just a place to sleep for her. Home was, and would forever be, a weathered house by a mountain lake.

As Jonah skillfully navigated through traffic to her new—and she fervently hoped—temporary living space, Cheney read her copy of Jade's email regarding the move. A suitcase had been placed in Cheney's apartment by the cleaning crew and a Cheney 'look-alike' had been installed there as well. At some point yet to be determined, she would exit, suitcase in hand, and be taken to the airport.

"Look-alike?"

She didn't realize she'd voiced her doubt aloud until Jonah answered with a shrug.

"Suitably broad-brimmed hat tilted to the right angle, face averted from likely camera locations, the right clothes on the right shape," Jonah elaborated. "If anyone is watching or listening, Jade will have made sure this person can pass. And someone will be watching. They already are. You can bet on it."

"Destination?"

He shrugged. "Jade didn't specify and may still be working on that aspect. My guess is our decoy will be on a private plane to some undisclosed tropical island location with a suitcase full of swimsuits and a complete vacation wardrobe in just her size."

"Unlimited expense account?" Cheney's smile was faint. Most girls' dream would be her nightmare.

Jonah shrugged. "Not unlimited but probably way over her monthly salary."

* * *

They'd barely settled into the apartment—richly furnished but not at all in Cheney's taste—when Jade arrived with her laptop and a canvas tote filled with charcuterie, cheeses, and crackers. She slanted a look at Cheney as she retrieved the last items from the depths … a corkscrew and a bottle of Cabernet Sauvignon.

Cheney thought longingly of her shot glass and her bottle of aged single malt but decided to hold her tongue. Jade was capable of packing it all away if she heard a single word that didn't sound like thank you. She was also kind enough not to remind Cheney of the plate she'd fixed for herself in the conference room earlier then ignored. Instead, she pulled saucers and wine glasses from a cabinet in the dining area and placed them on the coffee table with the food. She touched Cheney's hand and said, "Food, then wine."

"I know." Cheney placed a few things on a saucer then pushed it aside with a nudge of her elbow and filled her wine glass. "So, what's next?"

"For you? Shopping."

Cheney groaned. Another of her nightmares.

"Don't worry. You won't even have to leave this building. The couturier—Eugene Franks—is coming to you. And Jonah?"

He glanced up from his laptop. "Yeah?"

"I've got it from here," she gave him a sly glance, "unless you want to stay and help pick out a few things for a recreated Cheney."

Jade grinned at his expression, and Cheney noticed he didn't waste any time closing his laptop. He stopped at the door and looked back at her. "Try to behave until I get back." And then he was gone before she could throw a plate at his head.

* * *

Cheney closed her eyes a moment and gathered her thoughts back to the task at hand. Recreated, Jade had said. "So, who am I?"

"Legit question. When you step on that plane, no one. When you emerge on the other side of the equator, you'll be Charlsey. No last name but plenty of style, beauty, and charisma."

Cheney opened one eye and snorted in faint amusement. "I own a mirror." But, when Jade's team finished with her, she knew she'd have it all. Whether or not that would be enough was anyone's guess. She tried to relax but failed.

Jade must have sensed her restlessness. "We have everyone and everything moving as quickly as possible, you know that."

"I know." All Cheney wanted was for them to finish and let her do her job her way. Preferably soon. Preferably alone.

As if reading her mind, Jade murmured. "We're a team, Cheney. We're family, and we're going to nail these bastards. Marcus is working on the set-up and your personal security in Buenos Aires."

Cheney nodded. Argentina was as good a jumping off place as anywhere. As long as it was by plane, she amended that thought. She'd traveled most of the Pan-American highway system while on a case a few years back. She didn't care to do it again, particularly not when time was critical and becoming more so by the minute.

"So, we somehow convince the Aguilars I want to escape my handlers, leave all of my fame behind, and disappear into America."

Jade gave her a satisfied look. "Good. I knew you were opening the documents I sent, but I wasn't sure you were bothering to read them."

"Oh, I'm reading them. I'm just not sure I'll be as good at dramatic acting as you seem to think." Cheney didn't like a thing about the script Jade had created for her. Or, rather, for her and Jonah.

For a moment, Jade just sat and looked at her. "Kidding, right?" Her voice was soft as she shook her head. "For years you've pretended you're not in love with Jonah. You're good enough even he hasn't figured it out, and Jonah's damned good at seeing through pretenses. That part, at least, you won't have to pretend. The rest you'll handle just fine." Jade slanted her head to one side. "You'll be everything you need to be. Monied, flashy, spoiled, stunning. The Aguilars will salivate at the prospect of the windfall you'll be for their operation."

Cheney felt her face flame, then pale as Jade talked. "When do we leave?" she asked, leaving the rest of Jade's comments on the table.

"Soon."

Cheney shook her head at the noncommittal answer. "Not soon enough. I could have been there by now," she said, staring at her phone, at yet another email from Jade. "I need to be boots on the ground."

"We're still gathering intelligence. Jonah and Colter are both convinced there's something more than we know going on with the Aguilar family and their connection to the Flannery brothers. I agree, and the more we learn in advance, the safer you'll be."

Cheney felt Jade's gaze fixed on her but pretended she didn't. Jade was entirely too intuitive. A lot like Jonah. Hell, a lot like all of them.

Chapter Nine

Jonah made a stop by his apartment, long enough to toss what little he thought he might need into his bag, hopefully long enough to let Cheney settle into the inevitability of Jade's plan. They would be stepping into their roles soon. Cheney's disguise would be the more dramatic, his less so but with a completely different wardrobe.

While he wasn't haunted by the memory of Angie, there were reminders enough to bring her to mind as he walked through the living room and into the master bedroom. It was Angie who had replaced the original chunky, designer furniture throughout with more timeless pieces made of rosewood. He hadn't much cared either way. More recently she'd been looking at new drapes.

He stepped into the bathroom and grabbed his toiletry bag. Angie had left her mark there as well, in the plush bath towels and a scented candle on the long counter. After a moment's hesitation, he took the long-cold candle and dropped it in the trash.

He'd disappointed her, and he was sorry for that—but not for any of the decisions he'd made regarding Cheney. He couldn't be. He'd fought the attraction as long as he could, and—while he was fighting it—she'd grown into a woman. One he couldn't, didn't want to, move past.

Placing his things near the door, he went to his desk, flipped open his laptop, and dove into the files that waited for him.

An hour later, he lifted his gaze from the notebook to the laptop screen in front of him. He tapped his pen against the edge of the table, the pen with which he'd made not one mark in the notebook.

He'd been skeptical when Jade's financial whiz kid hadn't found a single sketchy entry, so he'd begun reviewing the data Jade had forwarded. The whiz kid wasn't wrong. The Aguilar brothers were making a decent, even slightly better than decent, living under the current free trade agreement between the United States government and several small Central American countries. The goods listed were all legit and inspected by a wide variety of agents over a fairly lengthy period of time. No way could there be that many federal inspectors involved in any kind of international trade scheme over that many years. And, once on this side of the border, the scrutiny continued, if not intensified. Every questionnaire was completed, every 'i' had been dotted, every 't' had been crossed. Signatures were verified, names were validated, not just for the Flannery warehouses but for several others, which were rented and utilized for intermediate storage points. Most were smaller but a few were larger than those belonging to the Flannerys.

He glanced at the time, then at his suitcase and duffle by the door. He didn't like being away from Cheney this long, not after everything that had happened. But Jade's amused glance had been sufficient warning for him to stay away while the fancy clothes designer asked Cheney to change clothes again and again. No way in hell was he walking into that scene. Cheney was safe with Jade. Even antsy as he was, he knew that.

But, when he refocused his attention on the information in front of him, nothing changed. He leaned back and frowned.

His phone alerted him again. He'd ignored several calls since he'd started. He didn't ignore this one. No one ignored Marcus Slade, especially not his family.

"Angie came by my office to say goodbye. She seemed fine. Already found another position, but ... are you sure about this, son?"

"I'm sure, Dad. It wasn't working."

Marcus grunted softly. "It may not work with Cheney, either."

Jonah shrugged, realized his dad couldn't see the gesture and said, "I don't expect it, too. Nothing works with Cheney. All I'm trying to do at this point is keep her alive in spite of herself."

"We all are, son ... we all are."

Time to change the subject. Jonah leaned back in his chair. "At the moment I'm going through the Aguilars' financials. Nothing's making sense. I can't find anything that so much as hints at probable cause for a turf war between the Aguilars and the Flannerys. From the first, it was business all the way."

"Maybe something that Cheney's father saw, said, or did put a torch to their business dealings, even if only temporarily."

"Nothing that Cheney can recall." Jonah felt certain she'd been honest about that.

"Likely nothing she would've been privy to … but something," Marcus insisted.

"Always a possibility," Jonah admitted. "But, the other, even greater oddity is that, after everything was said and done, it *was* only temporary. After her father was murdered, after Cheney was kidnapped, after Kell died of injuries trying to prevent that kidnapping, the two remaining Flannery brothers returned to business as usual with the Aguilars. It doesn't make sense."

"Not yet. But at some point, it will. There's always a reason why people do what they do," Marcus reminded. "Keep digging, son. And I will, too."

Marcus broke the connection and Jonah laid the phone down while his mind considered the next unknown in the equation. What had triggered the disappearance of Quinn and his family a full decade after Jonah brought Cheney home to New Mexico? What had brought the Aguilars to Albuquerque, to Old Town? Why beat an old woman to death trying to get to Cheney? What did they *think* Cheney knew? And *did* she?

That questioned bothered Jonah the most. Was Cheney keeping secrets? After all these years, did she still not trust them? Not trust him?

Tossing the pen aside, he pushed the chair away from the table and got to his feet. He rubbed the back of his neck. Anger wouldn't answer any of these questions. Anger wouldn't convince Cheney that she—and whatever she knew—was safe with him. And always had been. But damned if he knew what would.

* * *

Jonah wasn't in the best of moods when he finally walked back into the apartment that Jade had confiscated for their groundwork. His mood took a deeper dive at the sight of the man crouched in front of Cheney, the loose material of her blouse bunched in one hand just below her breast. The fact that Jonah was smart enough to know a fitting was in progress didn't do a damned thing to mitigate his irritation.

Cheney's cool gaze watched him as he crossed the room to take a chair beside Jade.

"What do you think?"

Since he was pretty damn sure Jade wouldn't care to hear what he really thought, he shrugged. "I'm not wild about the contacts." Cheney's eyes looked as much gray as blue from where he sat. "But, as a disguise, what you've got going looks solid enough. Still need to do something with that hair." He rubbed his jaw, "Maybe heavier on the makeup. At first glance, she could pass for a boy."

"That's the goal."

Startled, he glanced her way for a moment. "She's going to be passing as a guy?"

"It's … complicated," Jade admitted.

He grunted. "Uncomplicate it for me."

"Eden had a really good idea. And don't glare at me. She's inventive and sometimes outside the box, it's true, but she's damned good."

Jonah couldn't argue the point since he'd told Cheney much the same. "I'm listening."

"You're going in guns blazing, so to speak. All the limelight … all the fanfare … all eyes on you."

"That part I like. If we try to sneak in, we're immediately suspect."

"And if you go in introducing a female model as the newest craze, there's too much, too many identifiable features and aspects we can't change to any appreciable degree."

Jonah nodded, still willing to follow the line of reasoning, still watching Cheney's every move.

"Honestly, acting on Eden's first instructions, we'd intended strategic padding of certain aspects but we got a hold placed on wardrobe from her at the last minute. And darn if I don't think she's nailed it again." Jade gave a small, satisfied smile as Cheney slid a pair of tight leather pants under the voluminous shirt. "Eden picked the name Charlsey because it's close enough to Cheney that she'll grow accustomed to answering and because, if anyone slips, it will be easier to recover. We *kept* Charlsey because it will work for male or female."

Jonah turned and gave Jade a solid look, not bothering to hide his thoughts.

"It will work," Jade insisted. "We'll fix the hair color, of course, but we'll keep it even shorter for the duration. We won't say if she's male or female. Articles we've planted and will use going forward, will use both pronouns, switching from one to the other throughout. She'll model clothes for both and look perfectly natural either way. Her makeup will match whatever she's modeling. One event she'll appear all male. Another she'll appear all female. And, some, she'll be both, switching back and forth effortlessly."

He raised a brow. "Effortlessly?"

"Trust me, she's been doing it for a couple hours. It

really does look effortless for her. Instead of trying to guess who she is and where she came from, her audience will be focused on guessing is she male or is she female. The other two questions will be a distant second and third."

The couturier shifted his focus to a pile of fabrics and what appeared to be half-finished garments. Giving a dismissive flick of his hand toward Cheney, he tossed some things aside and begin sorting others into piles. Cheney immediately turned her attention to an attractive older woman with a clipboard who touched her arm lightly.

Jonah let his gaze follow Cheney as she followed the directions of the woman and strode across the room, pivoted, and strode back, sliding a sideways, arrogant glance at the woman who smiled back at her, pleased with her silent acting. In Jonah's opinion, Cheney wasn't acting. She was pissed and not bothering to hide it.

Jonah gave the choreographer a nod. "Who is she?"

"Lauren. She was a top model for some fancy, and damned expensive, clothing lines on the east coast. Married into the family a few years back and walked away from all of it, but her skillset comes in handy from time to time."

He shifted his attention back to Cheney and thought damned if his mother wasn't right. Again. It wouldn't be easy. It would likely be just as dangerous. But it might, just might, give them enough of an edge to do what they needed to do without Cheney being identified by either the Aguilar brothers or by Declan Flannery. He hoped eventually to be able to trust Declan enough to bring him in but ... not just yet.

And the fact remained, he'd still rather do all of this without Cheney being involved in any way, without having to protect her, without having to think about her every moment, without being close enough to touch her.

* * *

After another grueling hour or two, the couturier left with an armload of garments to be altered. The woman with the clipboard whose name Cheney couldn't remember followed on his heels. And Cheney, Jade, and Jonah returned to the conference room in the Welles Enterprises Building.

An informal dinner was brought up for anyone hungry, because work would continue late, Jade said by way of explanation. Eden and Marcus joined them as did their top news release writer. Zander Winstock was of average height and slender build, his hair an early grey and almost the same color as his eyes. Cheney went with early because of his unlined face but knew that could be the work of a very skilled plastic surgeon.

Eden moved to the sideboard and filled her plate with the variety of things that were available. The deep blue of her charmeuse pantsuit brought out the color of her eyes. Cheney had no idea of her true age, but she was certain Jonah's mother didn't look it. Eden turned and glanced at those in line behind her. "Someone, make Cheney eat, please. The next few hours will be intense."

Cheney rolled her eyes, grabbed her plate, and stood with more irritation than enthusiasm. Hell, the *last* few hours had been intense. Jade was intense.

The room was quiet of all but pleasantries until the end of the meal when Eden nodded her head at Zander. "Fill us in on what you've been doing, what's done, what isn't."

"I've created an older social media account and a newer one as you requested. Once we finish the photography session, they'll be complete with Charlsey's background and the early years of her career documented through old newspaper and magazine clippings, with links to fake sources we've used for other missions."

"What photographer?" Cheney asked suspiciously.

"That would be me," Zander said with a wink. "I'm a man of many talents. But we won't bother with that until tomorrow after your hair appointment. Be sure you get plenty of sleep as soon as we're done here tonight. Makeup can do a lot, of course, but…" he shrugged and glanced toward Jade. "All of the garments won't need to be finished, but we'll need a good variety. Make sure there's a mix of colors and fabrics in the finished ones."

"When we talked this morning, you said something about a cheat sheet," Marcus commented.

"A critical piece with this sort of deception. I've created a document for all of you really, but especially Charlsey and Jonah." Zander turned his attention to them, glancing from one to the other. "The sheet of bullet points will be what you need to memorize." He shrugged. "Jonah will need to be the blunt, outspoken of you. Charlsey, you can, of course, always choose to decline to answer questions from reporters, a softly spoken curse, a stuttered breath, quick eye-blinks, all make emotional connections they understand as the question being too painful to answer. Reporters always play on that kind of thing which will help create the façade without them even meaning to."

Cheney gave Jonah a look. That kind of emotional acting was not one of her strong points.

"But," Zander continued, "an answer, one that can be verified—as all of them can be—is always the better course."

"Charlsey, I've given you a background story of older parents who adopted you but are now deceased, a modeling audition at fourteen, in which you didn't impress the judges, and another at sixteen, still without any noticeable recognition but where you caught the eye of the up-and-coming agent wise enough to train you with small, in-store gigs until you were good enough to burst upon the industry."

"I'm Cheney," she reminded him quietly.

"Not anymore," Eden inserted just as softly. "Not to me and not to anyone in this room. Not if you want to survive as much as we want you to."

Eden's gaze held Cheney's until she took a deep breath and nodded.

Zander picked up as if there'd been no interruption. "I'll go back a few years and begin dropping stories here and there on those fake sources, sparse and scattered at first, then building steam slowly. Nothing that would have captured attention at the time but easy to find and follow the trail now."

"That would only be if someone is suspicious, right?" Cheney asked.

Zander stared at her for a moment. "Charlsey, you're about to drop into a level of stardom few people dream of attaining. People on nearly every continent, fascinated by your startling success, will be digging into your past." When she just stared back at him, he added, "Think Karlie Kloss."

"You can't create a supermodel from nothing!"

Zander lifted his brow but held his tongue.

Cheney turned to Eden. "And you can't possibly think this is a good idea?"

Eden gave a faint smile. "As a matter of fact, I do. Especially since it was my idea."

Cheney threw her napkin onto her plate in exasperation

and twisted in her chair to look at Jonah. "You have to agree that this is crazy."

His gaze steadied her. She could tell by his calm control that he agreed. "On the contrary. It's brilliant." Well, hell, she thought.

Jade sighed. "Don't scowl, Charlsey. You'll crease your brow, and your agent won't be happy."

"What agent?' She waved a hand in the air. "Never mind. He ... this agent ... doesn't even know me."

"Don't be sexist," Eden admonished with a wink as she walked to the sidebar and poured herself a glass of wine. "She."

"You know her?"

Eden turned to face the table, leaning one hip against the bar. "I do, and so do you. Angel Whittaker."

That was the point at which Cheney decided they were, indeed, crazy. Every last one of them. Angel Whittaker ... the face of apple pie America but deadly with a knife ... a talent agent? And for a model no less? Cheney got to her feet, not even sure what she was about to do, but then Jonah's father rose and held out his hand to her. "Let's walk a bit, shall we?"

She stood in indecision, then released the breath she'd been holding and took Marcus's hand. To do anything else would have been ruder than even she could be. And that, being rude when the moment called for it, was something that had never bothered her.

They strolled the length of the corridor, where Marcus stopped at glass doors that separated them from a skylight-covered atrium. He didn't bother to open them, and he didn't speak. He just stood there so Cheney did the same.

The stiffness in Cheney's shoulders slowly eased as the silence flowed around them. As if he'd sensed her inner turmoil ebbing, Marcus patted the hand he'd placed on the crook of his arm. "We're all very aware that we're sending you into serious danger."

Cheney stared at the flowering vines with their colors muted by lamplight. "I'm used to danger," she reminded him. "It's my job."

"And you do it well, but ... it's our job to protect ... and we do that well." He paused before adding, "I know—hell, we all know—how much you hate a spotlight of any kind. You'd rather slide in, shoot the head off the serpent, and slide back out, but that won't work with this case, Cheney."

She hesitated to ask, "How do you know? How do you know it won't work?"

"Because there's at least two heads to this snake ... maybe more."

And that was exactly what she was afraid he'd say.

None of this was going according to plan ... not her plan anyway. With that acknowledged, she asked what she'd been longing to ask. "Why are you and Eden divorced? It's clear to everyone you're still madly in love with one another ... so ... what the hell?"

"What the hell, indeed," Marcus agreed. "I adore Eden but I got busy and complacent and stopped showing her. Eden has a strong inner core, but she needs to be adored. She positions herself as someone who doesn't care, but she cares deeply. She's ... not insecure, but neither is she secure."

"That doesn't make a lot of sense."

"I agree. But nor does life."

"Do you love her?"

"More than my next breath."

"When was the last time you told her?"

He turned to look at her. "It isn't that easy."

"The hell it isn't."

He raised a brow at her quick retort then gave a rueful chuckle. "We'll see."

And Cheney hid her smile.

* * *

Jonah watched as his father tucked Cheney's hand into the crook of his arm. "It's a lot for her to take in," he said aloud as they disappeared into the hall.

"Will she be able to handle it?" Zander asked.

"She can handle anything, but this isn't how she operates and right now she's mad. Her aunt is dead—brutally, cruelly dead—and she wants revenge. Cheney is fine with fading into the background and fighting in the shadows. Having a spotlight shone in her face … that's a hard sell for her."

"And a dangerous one," Jade said.

Eden walked back to the table and returned to her seat. "Cheney doesn't care about the danger." The words were in response to Jade but they were meant for Jonah who met her gaze across the table.

"No," he agreed, "she doesn't. At least not in regard to her own safety." But he cared. A lot. That's why, along with himself, Angel and her knife skills were the absolute best he could bring in for Cheney's protection.

Jonah's role would be as her bodyguard, the official one. Angel would be backup for places that he couldn't go such as restrooms and changing rooms. If anyone got the best of him, which he didn't intend to happen, they wouldn't consider Angel a hindrance—until they encountered her knife. She was good with a gun, as well, but she was unmatched with a knife.

As if following his line of thought, which she probably was because she was that damned good at it, Jade asked, "When will Angel join the team?"

"Colter and I will brief her first thing in the morning."

Jade nodded. "Good, I'd like her here to watch as Cheney is coached through a final modeling session. Hopefully by then most of the alterations will be complete on the garments that were selected for her debut. The remainder can be finished later."

Jonah stilled as he realized that Cheney and Marcus had walked back into the room. Cheney had stopped near the door to listen. Jonah's gaze searched her face but he couldn't tell if his dad had worked any magic with her. All she said was, "Modeling? More?" before sending Jade an apologetic look and a murmured, "Sorry." When Marcus chuckled, she gave him a faint smile, and Jonah let some of the tension ease from his spine.

"You'll be glad for what Lauren can teach you," Eden said. "This is all a kind of show business."

Cheney looked at Jade. "Will she travel with us?"

"Yes, to study the setups at each fashion show and help you with choreography. Zander, as your publicist, and doubling as photographer. I wanted Eugene for last minute adjustments and alterations and any necessary repairs, but I think we can manage without him. The leaner we travel, the better."

"Angel, as your agent," Jonah added. "Me, as your official bodyguard."

"I'll also be armed, concealed carry," Zander said.

Marcus lifted a brow at that, and Zander gave him a good-humored glance. "Just because I don't prefer pickup trucks with shotguns behind the seat doesn't mean I'm not part of the clan."

Jonah grinned. Marcus did indeed have a shotgun behind the seat of his truck. So did Jonah.

"There's one last thing to be decided," Jade inserted smoothly.

Eden nodded. "Your playscripts." Her glance moved between Jonah and Cheney. Jonah snorted, and Eden chuckled. "I take it you've read through them."

He had but—from the look on her face—he suspected Cheney hadn't. His gaze held hers as he nodded and said, "Lovers or married or best friends, with one of us in a same sex relationship with some unknown someone."

He caught the glint of wicked humor in her eyes and, glad though he was to see it, shook his head and chuckled. "We'll be sharing a suite so lovers or married."

"I think lovers is better," Eden inserted. "Married isn't the image we want for Charlsey." At Jonah's lifted brow, she added, "Willful and untamed. Maybe even a little off the rails at times."

"Well, hell," Jonah said.

And Cheney laughed at his frustration. It wasn't loud, but it was real and something inside of him eased just a little.

Chapter Ten

When her eyes opened the next morning, Cheney didn't feel as if she'd slept at all. Her hair was still damp from her shower when she and Jonah stepped into the elevator for the parking garage. She carried her third cup of coffee with her.

She suspected she'd need more than three before the day was over. She preferred her methods, preferred sliding in, as Marcus had put it, to cut off the head of the snake rather than flushing their prey with this elaborate charade. The fact that there might be more than one head to this serpent, as Marcus believed, didn't faze her.

She said as much to Jonah on the short drive back to the Welles Enterprises building and the conference room that had become all too familiar in too short a time.

Jonah frowned at the comment but kept his gaze on the street and the busy sidewalks.

"We want the head of that snake as well," he conceded, "but also the hatchlings and the eggs and every last one of their henchmen."

"The hatchlings, the sons of Ortiz, are now the head of the snake. I can eliminate all three of them, one at a time. There are no eggs." As arrogant as that may have sounded, she was confident because she *wasn't* arrogant, and she knew that they were. They were older, now, undoubtedly meaner, but not wiser, and they would always think more of their abilities than what those abilities were actually worth.

"They have wives and children. All three of them."

"So they do, but wives are insignificant to them, and the male children are all younger than twelve. The daughters ... they're nothing, less than nothing ... to the Aguilars. And, third, there are no henchmen, no cohorts, no one waiting in the wings to avenge them. There never have been, and there never will be. They trust no one but themselves."

Jonah stared. "You're talking about an international ring of smugglers."

"A ring of three," she returned calmly. When Jonah shook his head in disbelief, she shrugged. "That's what Kell told me."

He pulled to the back of the parking garage but left the engine running while Cheney talked.

"Ortiz was the brains and he trusted no one except his sons, and barely trusted them. The companies and contractors they used, the thugs they hired knew nothing beyond the one step they were to provide ... not the who or the why of it ... just the what and the how of that one step. When the brothers die, that ring—the ties, the contact information, who did what, all of it—dies with them."

"Including their connection with the Flannerys."

Cheney nodded. "Including that."

As interesting—hell—as fascinating as that premise was ... and he had to concede it was more likely fact than premise ... it didn't answer any of the questions circling in Jonah's mind as they stepped into the elevator.

The large conference table had been shifted to one side to leave the central space open. Jonah placed his briefcase on one end while Cheney moved to stand at a window where leaden clouds ruled the sky although the forecast was for clearing by midday. He watched her unmoving form for a while then flipped open his laptop and started back on the timeline that had more gaps than substance. As far as he could tell there was nothing to bridge the gap between his rescue of Cheney and the disappearance of Quinn and his family followed by Lina's murder.

He paid attention as Jade arrived with the choreographer, paid more attention when Angel entered the room. Angel gave him a nod and her rarely-seen smile as she moved toward Jade to be introduced to Lauren. No enemy ever expected the speed of a knife in her hand, particularly when her expression rarely varied from cool composure. A person had to be watching for the lightning to flash in her storm-cloud violet eyes to suspect what might be coming.

Cheney still didn't look thrilled with the modeling scenario as their cover, but she no longer looked angry. Jonah tilted his head a moment, trying to decide just what her expression conveyed. Determination, he thought after a moment and that, he knew, was about as good as anyone could expect. Once determined, Cheney wouldn't waver. He might wish she had a little more caution, maybe even a little more fear, but he'd take the determination.

When Colter showed up just behind Zander half an hour later, Jonah's timeline wasn't any further along.

Colter tagged Angel to follow as he crossed the room to Jonah.

Jonah let Colter do most of the briefing. Jonah listened and commented occasionally while his mind stayed with the puzzle of the things they didn't know.

"Cheney agreed to all of this?"

Angel sounded dubious, and Jonah couldn't blame her for that. "Reluctantly and, I suspect in her mind at least, conditionally."

"Conditionally meaning as long as nothing goes wrong that puts the team at risk, at which point she's subject to go rogue?"

Jonah thought about that term. "Rogue as in uncontrolled, no. As in independent, yes."

Angel nodded, a faint frown creasing her forehead. "I can agree with that. Cheney's never going to be uncontrolled, but she is independent as hell. All that means is we can't let anything go wrong."

Jonah gave Angel a look that drew one of her easy smiles, easy as long as she considered everyone within sight a friend.

In turn, she gave him a thoughtful look. "Why now? If the motive was revenge for Ortiz's death, as Cheney suggested, they wouldn't have stopped looking once they started. Did it take ten years to find her? If not, and I'm seriously doubting it would have, why now? Did they find Lina first, or did they find Lina because they were already trailing Cheney? And if not Cheney's whereabouts, what was the motive for beating an old woman to death?"

Those were all questions Jonah had asked himself, and they were all questions for which he had no answer. Yet.

Halfway through the morning, Colter answered a phone call then disappeared. Not long after, Jade messaged Jonah. Can you take Cheney out for a drive or a coffee or ... hell ... a drink ... before she murders Zander?

Jonah looked up just in time to catch one of Cheney's glares as Zander adjusted her pose for a different angle. Sighing, he nodded at Jade who was watching him from across the room. Cheney needed a break. She was either reaching her last nerve or the photographer was stepping on it.

Jade watched him as he crossed the room. Jonah gave her a wink, then tapped on Zander's shoulder. "May I cut in?" he asked politely as Zander lowered his camera.

"By all means," Zander said, stepping back with an expression that more than hinted at relief.

Jonah met Cheney's gaze. "Take a drive?"

"Is that permitted?" she asked sarcastically, then sighed. "Sorry. Yes, please."

But when Jonah reached to open the door to the hallway, Jade spoke as she read a message on her phone to them, "Hold up ... detour. Missy is ready for you downstairs."

"Missy?" Cheney turned back with a frown. "Alex always cuts my hair."

"Not today. Missy is better with color."

Jonah was careful to say absolutely nothing as they rode the elevator to the lowest level of the building. When the doors slid open, Colter stood ready, flanked by two armed guards. "Jade says this hair thing's going to take a few hours. Eden's waiting for you at the front of the parking garage in a fleet car. We've got Cheney until you get back."

As much as Jonah wanted to argue, he simply nodded. Colter was as capable as he was of keeping Cheney safe. He wouldn't insult him—or make himself look like a fool—by implying otherwise. For that matter, both of them knew Cheney was as capable as either of them … but that was irrelevant.

He gave Cheney a single glance. "Whatever occurs to you to do … don't."

He was fairly certain her teeth were clenched behind the smile she gave him.

Chapter Eleven

Jonah slid into the front seat beside his mother. It was a company car, but he wasn't surprised to find her behind the wheel. His mother didn't care for drivers. Not even Jonah, although she still tolerated Marcus in the role. He'd long ago given up trying to understand their relationship.

He sat silent as she eased the car toward the sealed entrance and the guard stepped to the driver's side. "The street's clear, Ms. Slade."

"Thank you. We'll be a few hours. Marcus is tracking us through my cell phone so we're covered from here."

"Yes, ma'am. Be safe." He tipped his hat toward Jonah and stepped back as the wide, steel doors opened in front of them.

Jonah waited as she merged with the city traffic before

asking, "Where are we headed?"

"Cheney's apartment … to pick up her lookalike."

"Colter could have handled this with you." He didn't like leaving Cheney's safety to others.

Eden glanced at him then refocused on the road. "He could, yes, but it needs to be you for the Aguilars or whoever they have watching. It needs to be you they see making sure that *Cheney* is safely removed from her apartment to parts unknown."

Jonah pondered that a moment. He'd like to have found fault with it, but couldn't. As usual. He had a strong feeling that Marcus had made the calls on this one. They were intuitive moves. Odd that his father was the intuitive one, his mother the cooly logical of the couple. Or maybe not so odd. Hell, he'd given up trying to figure that one years ago. Just as he'd given up trying to understand they were still a couple in everything except legalities. They worked in sync, thought in sync, entertained in sync. He wouldn't be the least surprised if they didn't still share a bed. But he never let his mind do more than skirt the edges of that possibility.

Still … "It's damned unlikely that they'll see us going into or out of Cheney's apartment building." Old apartment building, he reminded himself. Once this business was done, he'd ask Marcus to pressure her to stay where they'd moved her. His dad was a fair hand at reasons and excuses to get his way.

"I agree there's little possibility we'll be noticed at this point. That's why a small memorial service has been planned for Cheney's aunt on the plaza in front of her shop. Signs were posted and flyers were handed out in shops yesterday after lunch."

Jonah thought about the contradiction in that. The

plaza drew a lot of traffic. "Small?"

"As far as duration and personages…yes. No VIPs, no high-ranking officials. A small band quietly playing, friends dropping bouquets of flowers at her shop door, that sort of thing."

"And how exactly are we protecting our decoy?"

"Lina was known as a friend of the local police. They'll have a strong presence of street officers lining the sidewalks as they single file past her door with their bouquets. And we'll do much the same. Several patrol cars will be parked around the square, visible but no lights."

"Cheney's going to be pissed." And hurt.

"She won't. She'll get an email from Jade just as the event starts, explaining that a true memorial at a time and place of her choosing will happen in the future when we know she can safely attend."

Jonah knew Cheney wouldn't choose. Her grief would remain her own. She'd take vengeance and there would be anger, but the anger would be contained, controlled in order to accomplish her goal. Cheney was always contained, controlled.

One day he'd like to make her lose that control. Fortunately, that realization stopped his mouth along with his train of thoughts. The image it brought to mind was something to set aside for now and damn sure not a thing to discuss with Eden ever.

The guard waved at them from the bullet-proof glass building as Eden passed her card across the face of the scanner. When the bar lifted, she pulled into a guest spot between the entrance and the elevator. Jade had wanted suitcases visible from the street when they exited.

Before Eden opened her door, she looked at Jonah. "The guard service was instructed earlier to have all cameras facing streetside, the better to see if we've been followed or if, perhaps, the building is already being watched. You'll be sent the videos once we pull away from the garage."

They took the elevator to the fourth level where Eden rapped on a door near the end of the hall. The occupant didn't make them wait any longer than it took for her to flip the security peephole open to check. She opened the door with a quick smile that looked to Jonah to hold nerves or excitement or an equal measure of both.

"Come in. Please."

"Good morning, Layla. Eden Slade," she said extending her hand, "and, my son, Jonah Slade, to pick you up. The guard contacted you to give warning we were on our way up, did he not?"

"Yes, ma'am, and Jade sent an email last night with the time. It's nice to meet you. I mean, we met at my orientation a few years ago…kind of. You shook my hand, but there were several of us coming aboard."

Definitely nerves, Jonah thought as she rushed through her words.

"And as I recall, you had lovely shoulder length blonde curls," Eden said regretfully.

"You remember me! That's really amazing and so nice. And, this…" Layla touched the cropped ends of hair dyed to warm copper tones and flat-ironed into obedience. "I didn't mind. It will grow back," she agreed. "Besides this style will be fun to play with."

Jonah managed not to stare as she secured a broad-brimmed hat over her hair, shadowing her face. A family resemblance was strong through all three lines of the family, and there was no missing her resemblance to Cheney. It would be enough—more than enough--from a distance. The two women were of the same approximate height and weight. Up close, Layla's bare arms, while firm and toned, lacked Cheney's defined muscles, but that was to be expected. Few women worked out with the rigid dedication of a trained Slade Agency operative.

Jonah smiled at her. "It's good to see you again."

The hair style had thrown him for a moment, but with his mother's reminder of long blonde curls, he placed her with the team that provided backup security to local law enforcement during charitable events, whether city, county or state. She'd be trained to spot and report threats, capable of defending herself in a fight, but not trained to the degree of Frank's team. Not trained to attack. Not trained to kill.

"And we appreciate your willingness to take a special assignment."

Layla shook the hand he extended to her. "I jumped at the chance," she admitted. "I love my job but I love traveling, too."

"Are those your only bags?" He pointed next to the door. One appeared to be a makeup case, the other a medium sized suitcase.

Layla nodded. "Just the two." She had a purse over her shoulder and pulled a laptop case from the end table near the door as she spoke.

"That's not much luggage," Eden commented, with a faint frown. "We're hoping to have you home as soon as you'd like to return, but there's no guarantee it won't last longer than we anticipate."

"Oh, yes, ma'am, I know." Layla's expression turned somber. "Ms. Jade explained that this assignment is to convince whoever attacked Ms. Cheney's aunt, as well as the news media, that she—Ms. Cheney—is out of the country for now. As far as the clothes, with what you're paying me, I plan to pick up a few things for now and more for my honeymoon in December." Her smile came back. "I won't mind shopping in Rio de Janeiro one bit."

Eden chuckled. "Good luck finding a winter wardrobe in Rio this time of year."

Layla's attitude for the journey, as well as the role she was to play, eased Jonah's mind as it seemed to do for Eden. A forty-hour week, even an occasional fifty-hour week was one thing. Asking an office employee to take on an around-the-clock job for what could prove to be several weeks was another. And there was some risk here. Not elevated, and less than what she was trained and expected to do in her current job, but some. He picked up her bags and smiled at both of them. "Let's roll, shall we?"

* * *

As they exited the parking garage, Jonah's cell phone pinged and he opened the file with the camera and scanned through the multiple videos for several moments.

He took a fast look at the back seat before saying anything. Layla had her ear phones in listening to music or a podcast. Jonah felt a tightening in his shoulders. As much as he hated putting employees at any kind of risk, it was part of their job descriptions, part of the assessment they all went through and were trained for, and each assignment outside of the daily routine was always, always voluntary.

"Watch for a charcoal punked-up truck with the front tires jacked. He made several passes in front of the building in the time we were inside. Could just be someone looking for a place to park or waiting for someone to exit a building and jump in for a hot, illicit date."

Eden glanced his way. "But you don't think so."

"No. I don't."

"What happened to generic, nondescript surveillance vehicles?" she asked. "Because that's what you're looking for. Someone monitoring our movements, trying to keep up with what we know and what we plan. Trying to locate Cheney. All while not being seen."

"Take a look around ... these days bland stands out. Jacked-up, punked-up is the norm, especially downtown."

Neither of them caught sight of the suspect truck as Eden made her way skillfully toward Albuquerque Old Town. A few matched all but the color, but—as Jonah had said—that was the norm this day and time. As planned, she made a slow circuit of the plaza while Jonah visually confirmed the positions of each of his team on upper levels around the square ... a hotel balcony, the open-air seating of a popular restaurant ... blending as they yawned, stretched, scrolled through social media, less conspicuous for making no effort to hide, but still visible as they were intended to be and obvious to those who knew why they were there. While Eden parked, Jonah received a quick all-quiet message from each of the four.

Jonah stepped out and rounded the car, opening first Eden's, then Layla's door, reaching for the three small bouquets of flowers created fresh that morning. He handed one to Eden and one to Layla. Music, soulful and plaintive, originated from a band of musicians in the center of the plaza and drifted through the quiet streets. A uniformed officer stood on each corner. As far as Jonah was concerned, they were for show rather than substance. Educated and skilled, no doubt, but constrained by rules and regulations his men had no difficulty skirting when necessary.

They waited beside the car until the current melody finished, then walked together toward the shop that had been Lina's, the place where she'd been murdered. Jonah continued to scan their surroundings, convinced they were watched. Two more uniformed officers stood, one on each side of the door. Wordlessly, Eden then Layla placed their bouquets on the growing pile beside the door. Jonah did as well, then took a moment to speak with each of the officers, the longer to give someone in the crowd that moved in and around their car an opportunity to affix a magnetic tracking device, the better to keep up with their prey.

Not that he believed it would be necessary at this point. Between retrieving Layla from Cheney's apartment building and their stop at Lina's memorial event, anyone watching should be able to figure out their next step ... ostensibly to get Cheney far out of reach. And he had no doubt, they'd been watching. That, added to the radio traffic with the hanger where they housed the Gulfstream should be more than sufficient.

As they walked back to the car, his mother, as well as Layla, seemed more subdued and less enthusiastic about the work that lay ahead. Their hearts and minds were likely on loss of life and the grief of those left behind. Jonah was just pissed, ready to fight and ready to deliver justice for an old woman he'd never even met but that Cheney had loved.

Still, he wondered if his mother didn't feel a bit of that burn as well, as she executed the remaining turns through the city then hit the interstate toward Santa Fe with a burst of speed.

Other than an occasional glance at his side view mirror, Jonah left road surveillance to Eden while he reviewed the broad strokes of their plan yet again.

* * *

The plane had already taxied from the hangar to the airstrip, and the small crew stood waiting at the base of the steps.

Eden parked nearby and Jonah carried Layla's bags while she and Eden walked ahead of him toward the plane. The pilot was a Welles Enterprises employee. His small flight team worked for the private airstrip rather than the company but were familiar faces. He greeted them by name and watched as they welcomed their passenger. If anyone had so much as an inkling that Layla wasn't Cheney, it didn't show. Jonah wanted to take that as a good sign, that her disguise was more than enough for anyone who didn't really know Cheney—and few did—but he still couldn't shake the small feeling of unease. Normal, he told himself, all things considered.

Layla thanked him with a smile when he wished her a safe trip, then she followed the pilot and co-pilot aboard.

As they were leaving the airstrip, Eden's voice broke his concentration on the folder he'd opened. "What's worrying you?"

He thought about it before he answered because there was nothing. Not really. Jade had put together a good plan. A well-thought one. She'd provided airport authorities two sets of flight plans. The authentic one, filed with appropriate authorities late yesterday but not made available to the public, indicated Layla's plane would touch down in Brazil about sixteen hours after the plane taxied down the runway in Santa Fe. The bogus one, available to the public but not filed with the FAA, had the plane touching down in Tokyo within the same approximate timeframe.

On this morning's outing with Layla, their decoy, from Lina's memorial in Old Town, and then on to Welles Enterprises private hangar, they'd been discreet but visible.

The four guards positioned above the square had also been discreet but also visible to a skilled observer. There was no reason for the Aguilars to disbelieve what was in front of them. One or all of them should be waiting in Japan while Layla landed safely in Brazil. Every aspect was detailed and damned near brilliant.

He glanced sideways at Eden as he answered honestly, "Hell, if I know."

And, beyond that, he knew he still needed to get a jump on whatever havoc his cousin had caused on her way to brilliance … which he had no doubt the second part of her plan would prove to be.

Chapter Twelve

J ade had been right. It had taken the professional in the salon downstairs a couple of hours to gently strip the mouse-brown dye from her hair. Gently was Missy's word. The whole process was excruciating as far as Cheney was concerned. It had taken another hour for her to blend broad streaks of gold with something a little deeper than Cheney's natural color. The effect was striking. Cheney wasn't sure she liked it, but she'd definitely stand out in a crowd, and she supposed that was the goal.

After that, she was passed back to Alex and her assortment of shears. "Those streaks are perfect, and blended so expertly you won't even notice when the roots start to grow out," the stylist commented with satisfaction. "I'm just going to make a few angle cuts so that it lays best for what Jade has in mind." Apparently, even Missy and Alex knew more about what Jade had in mind than Cheney. The realization frustrated her.

Alex went to work with deft movements, and Cheney tried to relax. Only when Alex pronounced herself satisfied, did she reopen her eyes and take a deep breath. Because the hairdresser was smiling, Cheney did her best to look pleased rather than annoyed because her irritation had nothing to do with Missy or Alex. They were professionals, doing their job. More than that, both were family, as were many of the staff in the building.

She stepped from the chair and murmured her thanks, then did a double-take as she caught a glimpse of Colter standing to one side, behind her. She hadn't heard him return.

He glanced at her hair and nodded. "Cute."

She rolled her eyes, and they headed for the elevators.

* * *

The team spent the early part of the afternoon discussing travel plans and last-minute changes to their itinerary with Jade.

The plane currently carrying Layla to Brazil would be returned for servicing and readied for the next flight in forty-eight hours. Once they finished here tomorrow, everyone would have an email with finalized information regarding travel.

Later in the day, Zander gave an overview and general directions for how he wanted the photo shoot to progress that evening with a plan to finish the following morning.

"We'll start with you in jeans and tees, then shift to shorts and minis, and add a few bikini shots."

Cheney cringed at the idea of shorts and mini-skirts and bikinis, and Jonah entered the room behind Eden just in time for her sarcastic response. "Sort of like a pedophile conditioning his prey?"

She knew she shouldn't have said it and cut Eden a wry look as Colter said, "Shit, Cheney!" and Jade laughed then choked on the swallow of water she'd just taken.

Eden chuckled at Cheney's wicked glance. "You have to admit, it did sound a bit as if that were the goal."

Zander gave Eden a pained look, and Cheney apologized.

"Not in the least," Zander said firmly. "From bikinis we'll switch to evening wear and, no, I don't mean lingerie."

Cheney managed a faint smile and tried to ignore Jonah as he walked to the back of the room and propped one shoulder against the wall. Apparently, he'd also been to the lower floor salon before rejoining them. His hair now held as many silver strands as it did brown and his perfect vision was belied by wire-rim spectacles which looked distressingly sexy on him. Distressing to her anyway. She shifted her gaze and focused on the camera Zander aimed her way.

Ignoring Jonah worked to a degree until Zander beckoned him closer and posed them together. "I'll change the background so that you're anywhere but a conference room in a Welles Enterprises Building," he said by way of explanation.

"The backgrounds ... they'll pass for authentic?" There was a rare hint of concern in Eden's voice, at least to Cheney's ears as she tried to keep from brushing against Jonah as Zander angled them this way and that.

"With our software? Beyond a doubt," Zander assured her. "Most of them will be on runways or in front of a makeup mirror or on an empty balcony. Some will be exiting private planes, standing beside taxis … that sort of thing. In some, I'll include Lauren or myself or Angel. Many of them will hit social media in the form of blurred newspaper clippings." He rubbed his hands together. "Technology is our friend in this."

It was nearing midnight, and they'd made it to the evening wear when Marcus walked into the room. He'd stopped by hours ago to check on progress, then left to attend other business. A glance at his face stilled their voices, one by one.

As he stepped forward, Eden took one look and took the hand he held out to her. "Marcus?"

"The pilot reported a problem with the fuel. ATC has lost contact." His stance was as straight as ever but the lines on his face were deep.

"Where?" Jonah's tone was as grim as his expression.

"They were in Brazil's airspace … just below the Amazon … nothing much there but jungle."

The silence that fell was deafening.

Marcus cleared his throat. "Please, if everyone will be seated." He pulled out a chair from the table for Eden, then looked around the room, his gaze coming to rest on Jade. "I've forwarded the tapes from the hangar's security cameras along with several communications. The video just came through so I haven't viewed any of it but, even if the tapes show nothing, we won't pretend our plane going down was an accident."

Jade, who'd been pacing at the back of the room, while talking to someone on her cell phone, ended the connection and returned to her place at the conference table. While everyone found a chair, Jade stared at her laptop. Cheney saw her lips tighten just before she pressed a button on the remote and lowered the projection screen at the rear of the room.

In silence, they watched as two men walked toward the hangar and entered a side door, before disappearing from sight. Both wore the one-piece garments common to airport personnel from mechanics to ground control to security. All that was visible were the backs of their heads. Each carried a fuel can of some sort in one hand. The time on the tape was near midnight.

"Are the colors correct on those jumpsuits?" Jonah asked.

"Not according to this email from the firm's spokesperson," Colter said, busy on his own laptop. "Close enough to pass in the dark but not a match under scrutiny, and they didn't have the firm's insignia on the sides of the sleeves."

"What about the video from the inside cameras?"

"They're blank. Both—which are just inside the door— were covered by dark cloths, tossed from below and at an angle the camera couldn't catch."

"Why wasn't any of this noted by the person on the desk?" Cheney could hear Jonah's frustration turning to fury.

Colter sighed. "As soon as she's located, that question and a host of others will be asked. She left work shortly before her shift ended, breaking protocol by not waiting for her replacement," Colter said, still staring at his computer. "So far, she's not at home and not answering her cell phone." He leaned back in his chair. "That's all that we have from the security firm, for now."

Marcus squared his shoulders. "Jade, you pulled together a solid plan. It's still solid. We just have to make adjustments in travel and timeline. Take a moment to gather your thoughts and determine how fast this team can step foot in Buenos Aires. And what means, what route or routes, should be followed."

Jade nodded and turned back to her laptop. "Separately," Cheney heard her murmur. "They'll need to travel separately. Nothing else is safe."

Nothing else is safe. The words echoed in Cheney's ears as she got to her feet, fingertips like ice, heart pounding. The room fell silent as everyone turned to look at her. She tried to speak but couldn't get the words past the lump in her throat so just turned and walked from the room.

As she reached the door, Jade said, "Take five everyone."

Cheney heard heels in the hallway behind her, but she just kept walking until she reached the rooftop deck overlooking the town. By now, her eyes were flooded, tears running down her cheeks. If she could have locked the door behind her, she would have.

Jade crossed the roof to stand beside her. Cheney kept her gaze forward, looking out through the elaborate wrought iron railing that rose from the concrete wall.

They stood side by side for long minutes before Cheney said dully, "We have to stop. This has to stop."

Jade's sigh held a wealth of sorrow. "We can't. Even if we wanted to … and not one of us would be willing to walk away now. Just like the Aguilars took from you, they've now taken from us. And we wouldn't, anyway, because you won't and you're ours. We're not just going to stop them, Cheney, we're going to end them."

They'd taken so much, Cheney thought. Not just her dad and Lina, but Kell and she had to believe Quinn and his family as well. By now they may have gotten to Declan. She had no way to know. And now this. Layla. The crew.

"We're going to end them," Jade repeated.

Cheney took a shuddering breath, and together they returned to the others.

* * *

Marcus looked around the room, his gaze somber but steady. "We missed their level of ability, maybe even the depth of their determination. Cheney may well be right ... there may only be the three but those three have money, and they're spending it. There's no blame to be placed. We'll close that gap and move forward." He waited for nods, for acceptance, then shifted his attention.

First to Colter. "Assemble a crew to comb through that hangar ... look for anything that points to means, methods, and opportunities for sabotage at the airstrip and hangar. What we've seen may be exactly that, but we can't afford to take it as fact until we know for certain. With any luck, you'll find something that will lead back to the Aguilars sufficiently that we can use it to slow them down." He scowled.

Then to Jonah. "I'll ask you to be boots on the ground in Brazil with whatever local authority is sent to the scene of the crash. I won't pretend that will be an easy task. They may not want to bother unless satisfactorily persuaded. Offer whatever amount you estimate they'll find satisfactory and take whoever you feel you'll need."

"I think we'll be better served if I travel alone," Jonah said.

Marcus nodded. "I don't disagree, but I'll leave that decision with you should you rethink it. Once there, you'll be close enough to join Cheney and the rest of the team when they reach Buenos Aires."

Cheney straightened, wanting to speak but knowing

Jade was right. A glance from Eden, a shake of her head, had Cheney leaning back in her chair. They wouldn't listen, not any of them. Nothing would stop what had been started, not before it was finished.

Marcus caught their silent exchange and looked straight at Cheney. "We have an enemy to defeat. A common enemy. From the very beginning, our families have been as one, and we've been stronger than anything or anyone who has ever come up against us. We always will be … as long as we work as family and trust as family."

As much as she wanted to argue, she couldn't. Jade was right, and Marcus was right, and this family was everything to her, all she had left.

She nodded, and Marcus tipped his head in acknowledgement.

* * *

Jonah let some of the tension ease from his shoulders. He wouldn't have relished chasing after Cheney. Her promise to Marcus may have been a silent one, but she'd abide by it, that much he knew.

Across from Jonah, Colter opened his laptop and went to work on Marcus's request.

"Ready, Jade?" Marcus asked.

Jade nodded and looked around the room. "I've emailed each one of you a script … a background … who you are, why you are where you are, how you think and how you feel about every other person on this team. There are no scripted lines. Dialogue is on you to ensure it's as natural to you as possible. You'll all be globe-hopping for a couple of days so plenty of time in airports and jets to learn to be you. You won't be traveling together. Not now. There's still safety in numbers for us but only if those numbers are divided."

"Lauren and Angel, you'll leave in the morning as yourselves, make a swing through Sweden with a twenty-four hour layover, and depart there under your new identities. If your wardrobe doesn't align with your identity, buy what you need. You'll be in several airports that I know have top-notch clothing lines. Don't skimp. You'll need plenty to impress the staff at the venue I've rented for the next two months."

Lauren lifted one brow. "Two months?"

"Appearances are everything," Jade reminded. "With luck, you'll all be done and out in less than a week. A lot depends on how swiftly the Aguilars respond ... if they respond ... to the message they'll get when all of you are in place.

"Charlsey, you and Zander will leave a day after Lauren and Angel. You have tickets on an early morning commercial flight out of Sunport. You'll overnight in Miami, then take another commercial from there. I've made hotel arrangements in São Paulo."

"São Paulo? Brazil?" Cheney had almost gotten used to being called Charlsey and supposed Jade had been right in insisting on that.

"Brazil," Jade said firmly. "It's going to take some juggling logistically but eventually the four of you will be on the same cruise ship into Buenos Aires."

"Wouldn't it make more of a splash if Charlsey traveled by yacht?" Eden asked.

"Yes," Jade acknowledged. "If we weren't taking over the entire cruise ship. A leak regarding her arrival will hit the media a few hours before the vessel drops anchor. Lauren and Angel will already have planted some seeds.

When she exits with Zander and Jonah at her side, no passengers crowding the deck or unloading ramp, we'll have all the splash we could want."

Marcus raised a brow. "I probably don't want to know, but how are you managing that?"

"I'm calling in favors."

Eden nodded. "Some favors are worth more than gold."

"At least no threats are involved." Jonah knew Marcus was only half joking.

During the exchange, Jonah had been watching Cheney's face, which she'd kept expressionless, but he could tell something was bothering her. Something more than the 'everything' which had already hit them without warning.

Apparently, so did Jade, who sent her a look of silent inquiry. "Problem?"

"You're not going with us to Buenos Aires?" Cheney asked.

"Not *with* you, no, but I intend to join you. There's a lot left to do before you'll be safe, and I can get more done here faster."

Jonah hadn't a doubt that Cheney could care less about her safety. Her focus was the fastest possible means to stop the Aguilars in their tracks, regardless of cost … even if that cost was her own life. And damned if he'd let that price be paid.

Little more was said as Zander, with Lauren's help, gathered the clothing and photography equipment.

Angel stood to one side, silent and watching. Jade shot her a questioning look.

"I'm Charlsey's bodyguard. I need to travel with her to São Paulo."

Jade took a breath and gave her a respectful nod. "I'm asking you to trust me on this ... she'll be safer without you in the short term. Once you reunite, I'm counting on you to protect her regardless of the cost."

Angel matched Jade look for look and finally nodded and all she said was, "To anyone."

* * *

Hours later, Cheney lay awake in the dark. Her mind shouldn't be on Jonah. She was supposed to be sleeping, according to Jade's directive. She had a job to do, risks to take, people to kill, deaths to avenge. Kell's, at long last, probably Quinn and his wife and children—and that thought gutted her—Lina's, the flight crew and Layla's now as well. The young woman's name haunted her.

Her mind was on Jonah, anyway. She knew that would change once she and Zander were on their way and the plan was in motion. It was a good plan, a solid one, better than even Eden knew. If there was one place on earth that the sons of Raul Aguilar knew as well as they did the California coast, it was South America. And if Jade's plan failed, Cheney knew just how to bring them to her. Jonah would be furious with her if it came to that and that mattered; it mattered a lot, but it wouldn't stop her. She wouldn't let it.

And she wouldn't let another death happen on her behalf ... especially not Jonah's.

Morning would come and, with the morning, she would force herself to be something she wasn't meant to be. No, she stopped the thought ... not force ... not if it meant stopping the Aguilars in their tracks, making each of them pay for every hurt Lina had suffered, for the loss of a young woman whose fiancé would be burying her instead of marrying her, grieving her instead of celebrating the beginning of their life together. Cheney would willingly do *anything* to make that happen.

The hardest part now, was waiting for morning.

* * *

Jonah's bag, packed and waiting at the door of the apartment, caught Cheney's eye when she followed the scent of coffee to the kitchen. Jonah leaned against the counter, watching as she came in and poured herself a cup.

His gaze touched her face, settled on her eyes.

"What time is your flight?" Her voice was husky.

He smiled, but it didn't look like a smile of amusement. "Which one? Jade has me bouncing like a basketball. Airport to airport."

"For safety." Cheney held her cup in both hands, needing the warmth of the coffee to combat the small slither of worry along her spine.

"Maybe. Or maybe just for her own entertainment."

They both knew that wasn't true, but she supposed it was better than any morbid what-if's they might voice.

His phone pinged and he glanced at the message. "My rental is here."

She raised her brows at that. "Rental?"

"Yeah. She went to the rental company unannounced and picked it up herself."

That slither of worry widened. Jade hadn't risked anyone putting a tracker on it. Did Jade think this was larger than the Aguilars or did Jade, no more than Jonah, believe her conviction that the brothers kept everything close to the vest?

He placed his coffee cup on the counter, once again holding her gaze with his. "You've got my number, Cheney."

"Jade said we should communicate as little as possible." It was as much a reminder for herself as it was for him.

He smiled faintly. "Well, don't call me if a fingernail breaks, but, if anything worse than that happens, I damned well better hear about it." His smile faded. "From you."

She nodded, feeling the tightness in her chest. "I guess I'll see you in Argentina."

He took a step closer, touched the knuckles of one hand to her cheek. "After Argentina, we have unfinished business. It's time we settled it."

He crossed the room and picked up his bag, giving her a last look before he closed the door behind him.

Cheney didn't move from the spot until she'd finished her coffee and stepped to the counter to pour another cup. Her phone sounded and she reached for it, expecting another set of directions from Jade, who seemed tireless.

Instead, the message came from Jonah. He couldn't have made it further than the lobby, she thought. He'd sent a link to one of the apps people used for sharing their locations.

She stared at it for a long moment, then gave up trying to figure out his motive. Slowly, she touched a finger to the screen to open the link and accepted the invitation to share.

Chapter Thirteen

Day was breaking as Jade turned out of the parking garage and onto the street. Cheney sat in the passenger side of the nondescript, gray sedan with horsepower that would put most dirt track cars to shame. The drive to Albuquerque International Sunport was short, and they let the silence lay between them. They were both fueled on coffee and little else, which wasn't the best start to a long day or to a conversation of any length.

The only question Cheney asked before they left was whether Jade had heard from Colter. She had not.

On a normal day, Cheney would have been boarding a private jet service, but only if their own aircraft were in service elsewhere. On a normal day, she would have arrived at the airport by taxi or one of several rideshare companies. Today was not normal.

As planned, Jade dropped her at the main entrance of the ticketing wing of the airport. As Cheney reached in the back for her bag, Jade called her name softly, and she turned.

For the first time since this started, Jade looked more stressed than hyped, more tense than angry. "Be safe." She hesitated then added, "Jonah will kill me if anything happens to you."

Cheney gave her a startled look then shook her head as she turned away. She didn't have a clue what to say in response to that, and there seemed little point in trying.

Her clothes felt odd, making her uncomfortable as she merged with the crowd. She was dressed in the current fashion, as a typical young person in jeans with several shredded areas. Wearing a long-sleeved tee topped by a loosely fitting jean jacket, also strategically shredded, she could have been boy or girl and any age. Fake earbuds completed the look of oblivion to her surroundings.

She wove her way toward the line at the far end, until she spotted Zander near a ticket kiosk. Jade had assigned him the role of weary parent and businessman. He gave her a look of relief, and she thought him a good actor, then immediately wondered if it *were* acting. Maybe he'd believed she might not show up.

Their bags were small enough for carry-on, and they stepped to the end of the line of ticketed passengers moving through security.

As they drew close to the conveyor, Zander nudged Cheney as if she weren't paying attention. Catching his wink, she gave him an irritated look of disdain that any recalcitrant teen would envy.

Zander shrugged and lifted his own bag onto the

conveyor, slipped out of his shoes and put them in the box. Cheney did the same, slinging her bag up as if anything broken could be easily replaced by a parent too wealthy to bother with their behavioral issues.

Zander moved through x-ray, gathered his belongings off the conveyor belt, then adopted a bored look as he stood waiting on the other side as Cheney followed him through.

When Cheney rejoined Zander with her well-worn duffle, he leaned close. "I'll suggest Jade not use this disguise again. You're enjoying it far too much. Jonah would be no end irritated to have to deal with you."

Cheney enjoyed that thought as they made their way to their concourse. They'd timed their arrival for the shortest possible wait and boarded the plane without fanfare. Zander stepped aside to allow her the seat by the window which she promptly closed as soon as she sat then turned to watch him while he stowed their bags in the overhead bin.

He swept a glance over the rows of passengers to the rear and stilled as he met the gaze of the man in the aisle seat behind them. Turning away, he made a casual, unnecessary adjustment to his bag, then closed the compartment before taking the aisle seat, leaving the unoccupied space—courtesy of Jade—between him and Cheney.

She'd already gathered the Bellamy agent behind them was also courtesy of Jade. If not Jade, then she had to suppose Marcus was even more tense about the forced adjustments to Jade's well-laid plan than he'd appeared the evening before. Cheney would've preferred that row also be unoccupied, but having an agent at their back was fair trade.

She was grateful for the space between herself and

Zander, preventing conversation. He didn't seem the chatty kind but long flights had that effect on some people. She was even more grateful the flight was smooth—long but smooth. Turbulence was not her friend. That was about it as gratitude went. She'd slept in bits and pieces through the night, but she hadn't rested. She liked Zander well enough, trusted him as Jade did, but she would have felt more comfortable with the freedom to act and react on her own. Nothing of which, she acknowledged, was Zander's fault.

The plane rolled to a stop and the fasten seatbelt sign went off. Not until the passengers in front of them and to the other side had moved past their row did Zander stand and step back so that she could leave her seat. She grabbed her duffle from the overhead bin, then he did the same.

She cast a surreptitious glance over his shoulder then faced forward and asked quietly, "Who's the dude?"

Zander gave her a hint of smile and said, "Just a guy I know."

It was enough of an exchange to confirm her suspicion that the man with the piercing eyes was with them without giving anything away to anyone who wasn't.

The flight and disembarking were as uneventful as boarding the plane. Their hotel accommodations, including the restaurant downstairs, were equally unremarkable. Cheney didn't mind and didn't question the lack of pretension in the mid-price hotel. She did question the distance from the port.

"We're ahead of the ship by a several hours and the area around the port is a hotspot for petty thieves. Lauren and Angel will board ahead of us, and the ship will leave port immediately once we join them."

She slanted a look his way. "Really…?"

"Jade made the arrangements," he said mildly. "Bite

her head off, not mine. I suspect she's not as worried about our safety as much as our announcing our presence with a litter of dead bodies."

The reasoning made sense, but this felt too much like being hidden away and she didn't like the feeling. She was used to being undercover, staying in the background, that was all part of the hunt. This, being the prey, and not going on attack in response grated.

Zander watched from the hall as she checked the room, then said goodnight as he pulled the door closed behind him. She had a feeling he waited in the hall until he heard the lock click into place on her side of the door.

Just before she placed her phone on charge, she opened the app to see where Jonah was now and a tiny part of her wondered if he did the same.

* * *

Regardless, she slept better than she'd anticipated and woke rested. By first light their driver was pulling as close to the boarding dock as logistics allowed. A quick glance at email on her phone over coffee had confirmed that Lauren and Angel had arrived and boarded around midnight.

According to Jade's script, as far as anyone associated with the cruise line was concerned, their team was part of a movie production looking at the potential of filming all or most of a movie aboard a cruise ship. They were to be given the gold star treatment but the crew were asked to remain as out-of-the-way as possible to ensure no leaks to the media. Even with only their handful of passengers, the ship still required dozens of crew members from deck to bridge. That was a lot of people to keep quiet.

With that said, Cheney thought Jade had picked the

perfect cover for their crossing.

The cruise ship was far more impressive than their hotel had been. Her stateroom was more spacious than she would've expected, with large windows looking out onto the ocean. She stood at her window watching the sunrise explode in color against the low-hanging clouds that thinned and drifted away like streamers.

When the engines rumbled to life, she stepped out onto what appeared to be a private upper deck outwardly facing the water, with a half-circle of cabins surrounding a large deck and pool inward. Zander was there ahead of her and she crossed to stand at the rail beside him.

Somewhere below deck, the engines rumbled to life and the ship slowly pulled away from the dock.

Zander didn't speak and, after a moment, Cheney broke the silence. "What if I get sea sick?"

"You've never been aboard a ship?"

"Nothing bigger than an old wooden fishing boat in a lake." She took a deep breath, pushing back on the ache of remembering. "I could be heaving within an hour."

From the corner of her eye, she saw his lips quirk. "The ship's doctor has meds for that. We won't leave you to suffer. After all her effort, Jade would have my head if I let that happen."

She thought about Jade's response to Marcus that she was 'calling in favors.'

"Any idea what good deed reaped all of this?" She gestured at the luxury around her.

"I do. I covered the story at the time. It was a good deed and good timing," Zander answered. "It belongs to a cruise line owned by a Spaniard whose daughter went missing a few years back. She was an exchange student in the US at the time and the Feds reached out to the Slade

Agency for assistance."

His words stirred different memories, ugly ones. "Was she found?"

"Living with her boyfriend, happily pregnant, and not the least interested in returning to the family fold. Unfortunately for her, she was only seventeen." He sighed at her look. "And, yes, the family kept up with her after she returned to Spain. At last check, she was again happily pregnant but this time married to the boyfriend and living on the family estate in La Rioja."

Curious, she turned to face him. "How do you know so much about our side of the business? Most of the press releases focus on the altruistic side of the company."

"That's just what we want readers to think, but we don't craft those feel-good pieces for the hell of it. My inner team searches for anything related to any of the three family names, the company names that appear in print globally. Anything negative or detrimental, we counter without appearing to do so."

"Meaning you don't criticize them or call them out as liars…"

"Not even if it's a blatant lie." He fixed his gaze on the coastline fading into the distance. "More, we don't even mention the original article or the person on the byline. Last year an article from Southeast Asia highlighted a young woman abducted from the side of her newly-affianced. The article also briefly mentioned that an entity from the Slade Agency was also missing. We quietly countered with a story of a young woman of Malaysian ancestry returned to the side of her aging grandmother who'd been her sole custodian since the death of the girl's parents a decade earlier."

Cheney nodded thoughtfully. "No mention of an

abduction or rescue."

"None. Our article focused on their reunion and the young woman and the grandmother. However, anyone following the story of the supposed abduction, anyone researching Malaysia or a missing Slade agent, would easily pull in our story to counter-balance."

"So, you're more than just a pretty face."

He gave a soft burst of laughter. "Much more than that, I hope. But I thank you for the compliments ... that is, if it's meant as one."

The glimmer of attraction in his glance was disconcerting, and she asked quickly, "What about the writers not on your inner team? What's their role?"

"They get the fluff pieces which are still good for the company."

"Fluff?"

Zander leaned a shoulder against the sturdy plate glass between them and the sea. "A ribbon cutting for the new wing at a children's hospital we funded, a school picnic at a city park where we donated an entire line of playground equipment, that sort of thing."

"Sounds like pretty important fluff."

"Not so important to the movers and the shakers ... but for real people ... yes, it is." He straightened and studied her face. "I gather you're not feeling seasick."

At his casual tone, Cheney let the tension ease from her shoulders. "Not so far."

"Good. Shall we check out the chef on this floating palace before we get to work? At least test the coffee and sample the breakfast? That should tell us how lunch and dinner will go."

Chapter Fourteen

By late morning, breakfast was a decent memory, and their team was at work. And it really was work, Cheney decided at the end of the day, far harder than any security detail. Only the four of them were in the auditorium which was typically used for performances during the cruise. The crew kept themselves scarce, as requested. If anyone managed a peek inside, it would appear they were practicing for a performance as had been leaked. They had been, of course, but not one that would become part of a production released for movie goers.

Cheney hadn't minded the effort, or even the details of it, used to playing whatever part was required for her to be an effective bodyguard. Since Zander wasn't looking at her with any particular interest, she'd been able to relax and just go with it.

His part appeared the easiest. All he had to do was lean back against a wall, camera in hand, and keep his gaze fixed on Cheney and his attention, as he said, tuned to anything or anyone who might pose a threat. That—the threat— was minimal in Cheney's opinion.

On the opposite side of the room, Angel did much the same but without the camera.

* * *

Jonah swatted at yet another mosquito as he studied the small building that had been pointed out to him as the local law establishment. So far, Brazil had met his low expectations. He'd flown into São Luís and been met at the airport by two men Jade had hired through a mutual acquaintance. All he'd known prior to arrival were their names and that they'd come with excellent references from trusted sources.

Jonah's requirements had been simple. There would be no violence if any other means was available, no grandstanding, no solo performances. If it came to violence, fists were preferable to knives, knives preferable to bullets. Jonah didn't want to make any announcements of their presence, at any point, beyond what was absolutely essential.

If looks alone could intimidate, these guys fit the bill. Large, bulky, chest straps hung with weaponry, their expressions as intentionally grim as Jonah's was easy. At least as easy as was possible for him under the circumstances.

So far, Zé and Tonho hadn't disappointed but neither had they encountered any difficulties as yet. None, that is, beyond the logistics of travel by river from São Luís to Marabá, where Jonah had purchased a jeep and hired a guide.

Unfortunately, their guide had shown a heavy dependence upon the flask in his pocket and Jonah intended to replace him before they ventured deeper into the jungle beyond this small town, if it could even be called that.

The police station was crouched between two larger buildings and with the interior barely more than a wide corridor divided in half. One half held two long and narrow cells, one of which was empty. The occupant of the other was a young man reading a magazine while lying atop a neatly made cot. He looked content to remain supine. Maybe because there was no room for a chair, and he was too tall to sit upright on the lower bunk. His head would have touched the iron brace of the upper, and, if he'd chosen to sit on the top bunk, his head would have touched the ceiling instead. His only other choice would have been to stand pressed close to the bars that separated him from the desk and the officer beyond.

The entire area, possibly fifteen feet wide, maybe twice that in length, smelled strongly of cleaning products.

The officer who'd risen from behind his desk as they'd entered the building frowned faintly as he struggled to understand what Jonah expected of him. But, expected was probably too lofty a term and too unrealistic a goal. Jonah spoke primarily in Spanish, which the officer understood well enough, but he replied in Portuguese which Jonah understood even less.

"A guide?" He rubbed a bristly jaw. "Into the jungle?"

Jonah nodded. "Maybe twenty, thirty miles. For certain less than fifty." He was targeting the area below where the last ping on radar had indicated the loss of signal from the plane. Even with that, distance could vary widely with whatever had caused the loss, sending the plane in various directions for various distances. He was betting that something had been an intentional explosion caused by the fake maintenance team caught on camera prior to takeoff.

"To search for an aircraft."

Jonah nodded. Again.

"Sir ... there are no airfields here. Not anywhere close to here ... maybe the coast." He frowned and looked seriously dismayed. "And two, three days have passed? No one—" he stopped abruptly. "I mean ... possibly, but not likely ... anyone ..." His voice trailed.

Jonah agreed with the belief the other man hadn't voiced.

"Regardless, we need to search." And bring Layla's body home, along with those of the flight crew. He held no hope that she or any of the crew had survived. And he'd given up any optimism of being provided an armed escort before they'd even parked the jeep. They'd followed the faint rutting of the road inland from the river, taking the same torturous route as pack animals and cutting vines where needed to open the path enough for the jeep. He'd been almost surprised to find a proper, though tiny, police station. "And we need a guide and to rent another jeep, if possible."

The officer rubbed his jaw. "This guide ... you can pay?"

Nobody's fool, Jonah lifted his hands. "Very little, if you want coin."

"A jeep will not be hard. A guide ... maybe. Cesar?" He looked past Jonah to the young man on the cot.

Cesar tossed his magazine to the floor and opened the door of the cell and walked out. He closed the cell door behind him and moved to stand beside the officer before nodding to Jonah by way of greeting.

"You pay me and I will allow Cesar to be your guide," the policeman said, "and to use my jeep, with compensation to me, of course. Cesar knows the jungle better than most. If he tries to escape, you shoot him."

Jonah exchanged looks with Zé and Tonho and got lifted shoulders in turn.

"Done," Jonah agreed. "We'll be back for him at first light."

* * *

Cheney crossed her arms as Lauren and Zander sorted through what seemed to her an obscene stack of garments she hadn't yet modeled. Worse, no two looked alike. She'd learned her movements from the speed of her walk to the angle of her chin had to be different for each item in the wardrobe. A jumpsuit of material so fine as to feel weightless called for a hands-in-pockets saunter paired with what Lauren called a reflective expression while an obscenely short skirt required an energetic walk and a mean-girl look. Cheney had seen that look all too often in her early days in California, before her father had given up and allowed her to homeschool online. It turned out, you weren't supposed to flip a girl on her ass, not even a mean girl.

Turning, Cheney caught Angel in the act of escaping to the deck and, with a quick glance back at the pair she'd come to think of as her wardens, she followed close behind.

Angel heaved a sigh, rolled her eyes, but counteracted with a faint grin. "Now I'll get caught and be blamed when you're caught with me."

"If you were any good at your job, you'd save me ...

get me away from those two."

"If you were any good at yours, you could save yourself," Angel countered.

Cheney twisted so that she faced the water and crossed her arms over the broad rail in front of her. She could feel the other woman's gaze on her face.

"Jonah can take care of himself." Angel's words were almost lost to the crest and roll of the waves. Almost.

"I don't recall mentioning Jonah."

"You don't have to. It's there."

Cheney considered a sharp comeback but ... this was Angel. They'd worked together, broke bread together, laughed together, and wept while cursing together. Angel had saved her life more than once, and she had saved Angel's. And Angel was right. It ... whatever it was ... *was* there. It was always there. That didn't mean she wanted to drag it out in the open and talk about it. The saving grace was that no one but Angel knew her well enough to know.

"Sooner or later, you'll have to deal with it."

Cheney grimaced. She *was* dealing with it. The only way she knew how. "Are you angling for a job as Maggie's assistant?"

"Dr. Byrnes? Good one," Angel acknowledged, "but it changes nothing ... and I'm not wrong even if I'm not the company shrink."

Cheney wasn't sorry when Zander stepped out and gave them a look. "Break's over, ladies." He gave Cheney a sympathetic nod. "Lauren's ready for your next set."

No, Cheney thought, Angel wasn't wrong but she'd much rather deal with Lauren and another stack of fashion wear than deal with that truth. So, she forced herself not to check her phone to see if the link between them was still there.

* * *

The plane had cut a swath in its descent through the vines. Cesar had led them unerringly, as they'd followed the glint of silver on foot, forced to leave the jeep about two hundred yards behind. As their small group had fought their way through the thick growth, Jonah had wanted to believe someone had survived the crash. Now he hoped they hadn't.

The tail of the plane hung suspended in the thick lower branches of a massive tree trunk. The nose was crushed against the ground. Even with GPS, Jonah doubted they would've found the wreckage had it not been near the same stream they were following. This was his first trip through the Amazon rainforest. He planned for it to be his last.

He'd done his homework on the flight over, knew what to expect. Or so he'd thought. Supposedly much of the rainforest had been displaced by Brazil's fast-expanding population, but there was more of it left, in his opinion, and it wasn't friendly. Since setting out, he'd heard the call of a puma in the night, seen snakes as thick as his thigh hanging in trees, spiders even larger. But, as hard as it would have been for Layla or the plane's crew to survive trying to reach civilization, even if they'd suffered no injuries, that wasn't why he hoped the occupants of the plane had died on impact or before. That honor went to the charred circle of devastation that encompassed the nose of the plane and the area surrounding it.

There was no possibility of survivors, and without heavy equipment, no way to retrieve anything that might be left of the bodies after the conflagration. Even the smell of death had been burned away in the inferno.

"Boss?" Zé and Tonho stood watching him in uncertainty. It was Tonho who'd spoken.

Jonah shook his head. "There's nothing we can do." But at least he knew no one waited in vain for rescue. He'd done all that could be done, which was find the wreckage and validate the murders.

All that remained was finding their killers and avenging their deaths.

"We go home?"

Home would have to wait a while for him but ... "Yeah. Now we'll go back."

Jade would have to figure out the logistical nightmare surrounding retrieval of the remains and whatever physical parts of the plane might be needed for prosecution. If they were lucky enough for it to come to that. Jonah's focus now was keeping Cheney safe.

Chapter Fifteen

Cheney stood at the window of her cabin as the cruise ship neared the dock. She was in full make-up, wearing an ankle length dress of a simple cut in shimmering jade. As anxious as she was to get off Lauren's floating torture chamber, nerves swept her at the thought of being in the public, camera lens after camera lens, for days, maybe even weeks to come.

As Jade had promised, Charlsey's arrival had been leaked to the press just a few hours earlier. A limo waited for them to disembark but that wouldn't happen until Jonah came on board. Cheney took a deep breath and focused her mind on the job ahead and, for her, that job was taking out the Aguilars by any means possible.

Although she tensed as she saw Jonah step on deck,

another part of her, the inner part, eased. The jungle hadn't swallowed him. He fell in step with Angel and they walked the outer deck toward her cabin. She turned to face the door and waited. Angel gave her usual single knock.

"It's open."

Jonah stepped in first, and his gaze went straight to hers. "It should have been locked."

Cheney might have made a smart-ass comment had Jade not already let them know there were no survivors on the plane carrying Layla to Rio and had she not seen the soul-sick weariness in Jonah's eyes.

Instead, she twisted her wrist away from her thigh so that the pistol she held ready was visible, and all she said was, "I'm ready," as she tucked the pistol away.

As she walked out, Jonah fell in step on one side, Angel on the other. Zander and Lauren were at their backs. By the time they hit the gangplank, a crowd was gathering and Cheney lifted her chin, glancing neither left nor right. According to Lauren's instructions, aloof was the word of the hour anytime she wasn't play-acting on the runway.

She tensed as a reporter shouted, "Charlsey!" trying to get her to look his way as he lifted his camera. A soft chanting of her name, or rather Charlsey's name, began in the center of the crowd and moved outward, growing louder. Jade had warned what to expect, but Cheney hadn't believed it possible to create an entire person—an entire *famous* person—from nothing. Those were fans ... fans of a personage they only *thought* existed.

"This is crazy," she murmured.

"I know, right, babe ... crazy good, isn't it?" Zander answered in character, although she felt certain no one could hear him over the chanting and the distance.

"Charlsey, where's your first gig in Argentina? Is it

here? In Buenos Aires?" Cheney zeroed in on the woman who'd shouted the question at her, then let the instinctive tension ebb, although it took some effort. Just another reporter, camera lifted, looking for that perfect shot. "No one's selling tickets yet. Not any venue. Give us the scoop."

Gazing across the small sea of faces, she wondered how they could get to the limo beyond without pushing their way through. She was certain that physical force wasn't going to be the answer.

As if on cue with her thought, a dozen army jeeps in single file rolled past the limo and eased into the crowd which yielded gracefully and without incident or so much as a murmur of protest. Within minutes, the jeeps formed a barrier between the crowd and the small group leaving the cruise ship. The drivers stepped out and stood, if not at attention, at least with shoulders back and a respectful stance.

The driver of the limo exited and opened the back door where Jade, sleek in a tailored suit, stepped out to greet them.

"I trust your journey was pleasant," Jade said.

Cheney gave her a look and left the answer to Angel. "Very much. Completely uneventful, and Lauren is a perfect sweetheart to work with."

Zander coughed while Jade grinned and said, "I knew she would be. Zander, too, I hope."

Cheney bared her teeth in the most damning smile possible and gestured toward the limo still running smoothly. "Shall we? I'm anxious to see our home away from home."

"Of course, but don't get too attached. We'll only be here a few weeks. We've cities and cities to go."

If Cheney hadn't understood that comment was for

the benefit of listening ears, she would've done more than show her teeth at that point. She wasn't any happier at finding herself seated between Zander and Jonah. Jade returned to the front with the driver while Angel and Lauren took the third-row rear seat.

The temperature was mild enough and the drive to their hotel was short enough they could easily have walked. Cheney said as much to Jade who shifted to look back at her. "Only if you cared to bring Angel's considerable skills into play."

Since they both knew that Angel's considerable skills involved razor-sharp blades, unerring aim, and blinding speed, Jade's meaning was clear. The area wasn't safe for a stroll. Cheney, of course, could take care of herself if her disguise allowed for either a pistol or a high-caliber rifle. It did not.

Cheney glanced at the elegant sign at the entrance to the resort. She couldn't pronounce the name but suspected there were plenty of well-paid staff who could pronounce it for her if she wished. She didn't wish. She wanted only to finish this job and return home. She wouldn't find pleasure in taking down the Aguilars. Her work was never about pleasure. But there would be revenge, and there would be closure. She needed—desperately needed—that closure, not just for herself, but for her father and Lina, for the Flannerys. And now Layla and the flight crew added to the body count. Cheney swallowed down the rising wave of rage. She was on stage, in full display, weaving the web to catch the Aguilar brothers. Catch and kill, she thought. Catch and kill.

The limo pulled to a stop in front of the hotel and staff spilled out onto the sweep of stairs. Jonah stepped out of the door on his side, scanning the scattered group with a hard gaze. Zander did the same on the other. Cheney would have rolled her eyes at the theatrics but, since no one was paying her the least attention, she just set her jaw and waited.

A moment later, she decided being ignored wasn't bad, not half as bad as being fawned over and beamed at by star-struck personnel. Maybe high-profile personalities weren't naturally ill-tempered. Maybe it was a byproduct of stardom.

Stifling a sigh, she waited with an expression of patience—if not the real thing—until Jonah extended his hand to her. She slid to his side of the limo and placed her hand in his.

His expression was less grim but that was as much as she could say about it.

"Is anything wrong?"

Jonah glanced at her. "Damn near everything."

And that, Cheney thought, was the first thing they'd agreed upon in a very long time.

Jonah looked across the roof of the limo to Zander and said, "Let's go."

* * *

In keeping with their extravagant entrance, Jade had booked the entire first level of rooms. Jonah hadn't agreed with that lower floor decision, initially. Too many entrances. Too many exits. Too easy for an assassin to slip in and out. Jade's reasoning had been the flip side of that coin. Elevators could be taken out of service. The stairways could be held by a handful of men with enough firepower. A well-set blaze could sweep through the upper levels in an instant, a bomb could bring the infrastructure down with no escape for guests above. These people might enjoy getting their hands on Cheney to even the score for their father, but Layla's death made clear their ultimate goal was to silence her.

Regardless, Jade was directing the operation. Jonah's role was to keep Cheney safe until the Aguilars were drawn into the open and taken in or taken down. Since Jonah didn't care what the reason was behind their hunt for Cheney, taken down would suit him just fine.

Lauren put them right to work, not even giving them time to unpack. They'd dropped their bags in their rooms. Jonah watched while Cheney searched her suite, and she waited while he searched his, which adjoined it, before they returned to the ballroom below.

Angel guarded the door at the rear, Jonah watched the stage from the door at the front. Zander stayed within a few feet of Cheney, and Jonah knew he was armed as were Jade and Cheney.

Even with all of that, Jonah couldn't relax and would have given a year's salary to have Colter at hand. But the Slade agency couldn't manage itself, not with their current caseload and the amount of territory they covered.

Cheney seemed different now. She appeared to have ceased viewing her part in the deception as some kind of punishment. She'd accepted her role and even mastered it. Her movements were purposeful and her expression focused. If Lauren asked for fierce, that was what she got. Jonah wasn't surprised that fierce was easiest for Cheney, but she also managed lazy and playful, moody, sleepy, the entire gamut of emotions. But when Lauren asked for sexy, Jonah stopped breathing as suddenly as if he'd been gut-punched.

Lingering images of a frightened sixteen-year-old

were wiped from his memory. Lingering memories of a vulnerable eighteen-year-old were swept away. Cheney was all strength, wholly determined, and completely woman. When she turned at the end of the stage, she lifted her chin as she caught him watching.

And difficult, he reminded himself, always difficult.

Throughout the day, Lauren made wardrobe changes and decisions while Zander snapped photographs which they reviewed at dinner that evening. He picked out several that he approved for his next news release and passed them to Cheney who shoved them on to Lauren without even glancing at them.

When Jonah's phone rang in the middle of that exchange, he stepped away from the table without fanfare. The call was from Colter.

"The report isn't stamped official yet but it's pretty conclusive. A contaminant was added to the fuel."

Jonah saw Cheney watching him with narrowed eyes as he walked to a door that led to a plaza at the center of the building. "Contaminate?"

"A chemical to increase the freezing point of the fuel enough that it overcame the hydraulic lines that are supposed to keep that from happening. The farther and higher the plane flew, the colder the gas tanks."

"We found the fuel can?"

"They left it behind. It was old, some rusted areas on the bottom. Probably lifted from somebody's backyard. Nothing to incriminate them and no chance of it being discovered someplace they live, work, or travel."

"Fingerprints?"

"Nothing. You don't notice them in the video but enlarged stills show they wore clear plastic gloves. Like the ones food handlers use and discard."

"Nothing to link it to them." Jonah rubbed the back of his neck but it didn't help ease the knot of tension. "Nothing to prove that fuel, or that contaminate, caused the crash."

"Not unless we can get the plane back to civilization. Even then it would only be a remote possibility any trace of evidence survived the fire, and, from the photos you sent …"

"Unlikely, bordering on no chance in hell," Jonah agreed with Colter's unspoken conclusion. "What about the missing security person?"

"Still missing. Never returned home or back to work."

"What's your guess?"

"Shallow grave someplace. She'd worked there too long to have been planted. Likely hooked up with the wrong person at the wrong time, never suspecting she was a target. Maybe slipped away for a hot date and thought no one would ever know. Maybe took a bribe, had her story ready for why she was called away, and never got to use it."

All of which pretty much matched what Jonah would have concluded. "Anything else?"

"Not at the moment. How are things going there?"

Jonah thought of Cheney's frustration with the elaborate orchestration of events and nearly laughed. Then he thought of how unexpectedly well she was handling things at this point.

"We're managing."

"Just a few days 'til your first public event, right?"

"Yeah," Jonah said, feeling that tension in his gut increase.

They disconnected the call and Jonah walked back inside to join the others. His glance met Jade's, and she lifted a hand at his expression. Conversation stilled around the table. "News?"

And he told them, watching Cheney's face as he did, seeing the sorrow and the anger and ultimately the guilt. And it was the guilt that pissed him off.

Jade must have seen it, too. That guilt and his fury along with it. She gave him a small shake of her head and spoke. "This isn't on you, Cheney. It's on them. The Aguilars. And we'll stop them."

Cheney clenched her hands on the table in front of her. "No matter what we do now, it won't bring them back … Layla and the crew. They died because of me."

"The hell, they did." Jade's eyes flashed with her own anger. "The Aguilars took their lives without help from anyone, least of all you. And they'll pay for it. We'll stop them midstride and they'll pay. I promise you that." Jade shoved her plate away. "Now, let's get back to work."

That first day set the pattern for the next few days. More than that, it set the tone for all of them. Nights, however, were very different.

* * *

Cheney's nightmare took Jonah by surprise, not that he would have been surprised to know she had dreams that were sheer hell but the slow, mournful sound of her weeping nearly undid him.

He stepped out of bed and slid into his jeans before crossing the room to lean his forehead against the door between them. He had no idea if she was awake or wept in her sleep, had no idea if she'd welcome his intrusion or threaten to shoot him. She was a damned good shot, one of the best he knew, but each time she took a bad guy down, he suspected a small piece of herself went down as well. That, alone, might keep him in one piece until she was sure.

He rapped his knuckles lightly against the door between their rooms and said her name softly. The weeping continued, and he knew with a certainty that she was asleep. He tried again, harder, louder. Her breath caught and then there was silence. He said her name again.

"Go back to sleep, Jonah."

Ignoring that, he knocked again.

"Damn it." The curse was as soft as the sound of her weeping had been.

Considering he'd given her fair enough warning, Jonah opened the door and stepped through.

She shifted until she was sitting up, watching him. There was just enough moonlight through slits in the shutters for him to see her against the headboard. "Go away," she said tiredly.

"No." He meant it. He'd be damned if he'd leave her crying. Instead, he sat on the edge of the bed and pulled her in his arms. Swinging his legs onto the mattress, he leaned against the headboard.

"I'll hate you in the morning," she murmured. He could hear her exhaustion.

"I know."

"He's dead." Her voice was soft. "Quinn, his wife, their kids."

He gave a small nod. He'd reached that conclusion.

All three brothers had come to New Mexico. They trusted no one but themselves, Cheney had said. No one left behind to guard their captives; therefore, no captives left to guard.

Whatever information they'd wanted from Flannery and failed to get, they believed Cheney could provide it. Or was Cheney—her location—their goal? If Cheney knew, she wasn't saying. That bothered him on several levels and left him with a lot of questions ... too many.

He held her until she fell asleep, and then he held her until dawn broke.

Chapter Sixteen

Cheney woke to sunlight streaming through curtains she'd closed the night before. Now they were drawn all the way back with just the sheers in place. Jonah stood staring out her window, coffee mug in hand. A second mug, still steaming, sat on the small chest of drawers beside her.

Cheney considered a smartass comment—even two—but wisdom prevailed. She sat and picked up the mug instead, studying him as she took the first sip.

Alerted by her movement, Jonah visibly tensed but didn't turn to look at her as he asked, "Nothing to say?"

"Not yet."

He shifted positions to face her, his gaze searching her face. "See you in a bit." He disappeared into his room, closing the door carefully behind him.

Kicking back the bedclothes, she took his place at the window while she finished her coffee.

The next three nights, Cheney dragged the thick comforter from her bed to the small but luxurious bathroom and slept on the floor amid that luxury. If she dreamed again, if she wept again, no one could hear her.

She often found Jonah studying her during the day. He probably wondered. But he didn't ask.

* * *

The first half of the fourth day went as smoothly as any day could on an op of this kind, at least in Jonah's opinion. With the team all too aware they were nearing the first major event of their sting, the intensity of their work seemed amped. He watched as Cheney barely touched lunch. She looked drained, but he hadn't heard any more restless shifting or sounds of mourning in the night. Lauren was pushing hard—hard enough that Jonah considered pushing back. He would have by now if not for knowing that any interference from him would make Cheney even more irritable than she already was. Besides, Lauren was only following Jade's directives, and it was Jade who called for a break at lunch.

"We're taking the afternoon off. We won't reach out to the Aguilars until after tomorrow evening's show, so the risk is no more than normal for any tourist being out and about on the streets or in museums. There are street artists and dancers, as well, and the local shops are damned good, too. Even so, travel in pairs."

Jonah stared at her. "You can't think this is a good idea."

"Cheney needs the break ... needs to get away from

this for a little while." Her gaze swept the room. "Hell, we all do." She took a deep breath. "The only risk above normal is if one of our newly created fans recognizes Charlsey. So, yes, travel in pairs, but either Jonah or Angel is to be with Charlsey at all times."

Jonah was watching when Cheney opened her mouth to speak but he was ahead of her. "I've got her."

Cheney leaned back in her chair, studying him. He didn't take that as a good sign.

Angel shrugged. "Then I'll be at the pool." She looked around the table. "Who's with me?"

"Me, thank God."

Angel grinned at Lauren. "Red or white."

"Red. I have a corkscrew and I'll bring the glasses," Lauren said, standing up and stretching the kinks from her shoulder.

"Make that three," said Jade.

Zander shrugged. "I'm taking a damned nap."

"You're not old enough for naps," Jade retorted.

"No, but I'm damned sure young enough for one."

Angel stood. "I'm going up to change into something really skimpy since I'm not on guard duty."

Her comment made Jonah wonder how many knives she had secreted in the sleek pantsuit she wore. She could have passed for a model right along with Cheney. It was an interesting concept, but he thought himself the wiser for not voicing it.

"Ready?" he asked Cheney.

She gave him a steady look then, just when he thought she'd opt for staying in her room, she nodded. "Is there a zoo?"

It was Jade who answered. "There was. The city shut it down some time back ... too many animals were dying. It's been transformed into something called the Eco Parque and, best I can tell, there are still animals, just not as many and they're in more natural settings. There's also a number of museums between here and there."

"I want animals," was all she said.

When Cheney went upstairs to change into street clothes, Jade motioned to Jonah to stay.

He lifted a brow at her expression. "Something wrong?"

She shrugged. "Other than everything? Too many unanswered questions."

"Nothing new there." All they had were unanswered questions.

"I know," Jade sighed. "My brain has been going in circles. It isn't hard for me to believe the Aguilars initially took Cheney from the Flannerys for revenge, but it's damned near impossible to accept it took them ten years to find her this time or to believe they even looked for her for those ten years."

"Which would mean the death of Raul Aguilar had nothing to do with Lina Navarro being battered to death." The suggestion didn't surprise Jonah. He'd been headed away from that possibility all along. The problem was, he didn't know where to look next.

"And, just maybe, her being taken from the Flannerys a decade ago had nothing to do with his ... Ortiz, I mean ... death, either," Jade suggested.

"Maybe, but Kell Flannery believed it did. The guy was gut-shot and bleeding out when I got to him." Bleeding out and too late for anyone to save him. But Jonah had pressed a bundle of rags to the wound as he dialed 911. Even knowing the man would be dead long before help arrived, he'd called. "Flannery knew he didn't have many words left in him so he made them count. The Aguilars had Cheney and it was revenge."

"Maybe revenge for something other than the Aguilars' father," Jade said.

"Maybe," Jonah mulled that over. "Possible, even probable, if you consider the recent disappearance of Quinn Flannery and his family."

"Circling back … just a thought … could Quinn have known about Lina? Would he have sent them here?"

"To save his family … hell, yeah. Wouldn't most men?"

"I haven't met most men," Jade retorted.

Jonah lifted a brow. "You meet them, but a handshake is as close as they get." He shook his head. "I don't think Quinn would have dug up an old card with her address on it. It feels like something the Aguilars might have found during a search, maybe killed him to make that search … but found it while looking for something else. I should have pulled the police report on the disappearance of Quinn and his family." Or asked Cheney more questions. Not too late for that, he thought.

"I'll have the police report sent to us. And you should cut yourself some slack. You've had a little bit going on," Jade reminded, "a few other things heavy on your mind."

He knew she wasn't only referring to their plan to topple the Aguilars from their deadly reign once and for all. His broken engagement hung between them unspoken, but Jonah wouldn't accept that as an excuse. It troubled him to realize that, after the first few days, he'd barely given a thought to the woman he'd planned to marry. Sure, they'd all been overwhelmingly busy, but—nonetheless—it forced a realization that he hadn't been in love when he proposed. He'd simply drifted his way there with a woman he cared for but, ultimately realized, he could live without.

Jade waited him out while he sorted his thoughts. The

problem was, he had nothing concrete. He pulled his gaze back to hers as he admitted, "Cheney knows something or the Aguilars believe she knows something."

"And, if she does, it begs another question," Jade countered, following that line of reasoning. "Does she *know* she knows something? There's hope there ... but only if she trusts us enough to confide."

"But if she doesn't know, or doesn't trust, we're back to square one."

Jade nodded. "Square one is simple. Take down the Aguilars and eliminate their threat. Completely."

"Might not be done as simply as it's said." But he'd get it done, whatever that took.

"Meanwhile you're going to have to push Cheney," she lifted a hand at his glare, "just a bit ... just out of her comfort zone."

"What damned comfort zone? She's been through hell."

"She's an agent of the company, and, Jonah ... She's not sixteen, anymore."

Restless, Jonah stood and paced a few strides out and back. He knew Jade wasn't wrong, but damn it, the thought of pushing Cheney felt wrong.

He turned to say as much just as Cheney came into view at the top of the stairs. He paused as his heart skipped a few beats. No, Cheney wasn't the sixteen-year-old girl he'd rescued. Nor was she the eighteen-year-old who'd asked him to kiss her. He'd known—known damned well— that if he'd kissed her, he wouldn't have stopped unless she stopped him. And he didn't trust, to this day, that she would have.

She walked toward them, glancing from him to Jade as if sensing she'd been the topic of discussion. "Is something wrong?" And that question, he thought with a rueful smile, was a full circle back to where his conversation with Jade had started.

Jade handled it as only Jade could, getting to her feet with a laugh. "Yeah, I'm not at the pool with the sane people, but I plan to remedy that now."

Cheney's steady look said she wasn't buying that carefree tone, but she shrugged and turned with Jonah toward the door.

Jade's voice followed them from the room. "I still think it's safe enough, but be careful out there. And back by dark or call me. I don't want to have to come looking for you. I've seen the throngs of people that hit these streets after dark."

Jonah wasn't worried about getting lost, or Jade having to look for them, but he checked the app on his phone to make sure he and Cheney were still linked. He wouldn't put it past her to silently break that connection.

She hadn't.

* * *

As they exited the hotel, they found themselves trailing a chattering group who followed a walking tour guide. The young man switched easily between English, Spanish, and Portuguese which suited Jonah just fine. Because with Cheney in street clothes and no makeup, they blended well with the unhurried tourists; they weren't likely to have panhandlers or thugs dogging their footsteps.

Despite her focus being animals, Cheney seemed perfectly willing to tag along in and out of several historic buildings and a couple of museums. By the time Jonah spotted the entrance to the Eco Parque, he was ready to part company with the tourists. The complex was at an angle from the direction they'd been walking, and he steered Cheney toward it with a hand at her lower back. She sent him a quick glance at the touch then relaxed when he nodded his chin at the sign.

They walked without talking, enjoying the breeze and the peace after the noise of the street. He could almost feel Cheney relaxing. The animals they passed didn't seem any more interested in them than they were in the animals. Cheney stopped to watch a group that were playing under a stand of trees.

"Those are cute. They look like oversized rabbits."

"They're called Patagonia Mara, and they're actually very large rodents." He chuckled at her expression. "You didn't care for the monkeys either."

"I've never cared for monkeys," she admitted. "Their eyes ... they look sad to me."

They chanced on a bench positioned near a lake and drifted toward it. The surface of the water rippled with the movements of small groups of ducks here and there. Most of them were shades of brown but some were feathered with touches of red or blue or green that flashed in the sunlight.

His mind wasn't on the ducks. Push her, Jade had said, meaning push the Aguilar connection, what she might have heard or witnessed.

That wasn't where he wanted to take a conversation with her. He suspected Jade was right and he needed to try, but when he opened his mouth what came out was altogether different.

"You were eighteen."

Cheney turned to him, confused at first but then she stilled. "You didn't just go there."

He clenched his jaw, had to force himself to relax, to answer. "It mattered, Cheney. Just eighteen."

She got to her feet and flashed him a look. "Every morning, I wake up knowing exactly what age I am. I knew when I was six and sixteen and twenty-six. That's how old I am now, Jonah. Twenty-six. I haven't been eighteen in a long time." Then she turned and strode away, and he scrambled to catch up.

When he did, she stopped so abruptly he bumped against her. And immediately stepped back.

"But I couldn't move past the sixteen-year-old I rescued. Everything that had happened ... everything you'd been through ... because I didn't get to you fast enough."

"But you did get to me. And I'm here, and I'm not sixteen anymore."

Her eyes had never looked more green than now as they held his ... then dropped to his mouth. He was in over his head and he knew it, knew he hadn't a clue what to do, how to handle the moment.

He took a deep breath, just as she said, "I'm hungry."

A moment later, he was once again scrambling to catch up. And not just physically.

* * *

Halfway back to their hotel, they slowed in front of the row of food stands and food trucks. Jonah would rather have kept moving, but Cheney studied them all, then moved to the window of one. He silently acknowledged there was still plenty of daylight, but the itch between his shoulder blades was troublesome.

He gave Cheney his order, then turned his back to hers so that he faced the street which, while not empty, was less crowded than when they'd started out. The waning of the crowds was typical between lunch and dinner. The night crowd would be different and would hold opposite ends of the spectrum when thugs rubbed shoulders with the rich and famous. Only rarely did that cause problems, but he preferred to avoid the risk than deal with the reality. And dusk would soon be edging out daylight.

He listened as she ordered his *lomito* and a *choripán* for herself.

Cheney took the bag and walked away, leaving him to pay. He followed her to one of the small tables that littered the sidewalk, followed but didn't take a chair when she did.

"Why don't we take these back to the hotel?"

She tilted her head at his suggestion. "It's early. I don't want to go sit in my room again."

"We could relax by the pool," he suggested.

"Or we could relax here." She unwrapped her sandwich.

Jonah scowled and took the wrought iron chair opposite her. "Who comes to Buenos Aires and orders a hot dog?"

"A hot dog with chorizo," she corrected him.

On a sigh, Jonah unwrapped his steak sandwich and started eating. He saw her sweep a glance across the area behind him and knew she would have his back while he had hers. He also knew they could be relaxing behind iron gates.

They'd finished eating and were nearing those gates when the steady itch between his shoulder blades increased. Even though he hadn't caught anyone tailing them, he was certain they were being followed.

As they left the street for the sweep of the hotel's entrance, Jonah sensed the motion behind them, even before the heavy thud of running feet registered. More than one pair. He grunted as the breath was knocked from his lungs by a blow between his shoulder blades. For a moment, he thought it was the slide of a knife, and dread iced through him at the thought of Cheney being left to fight them off, being dragged away and no one there to prevent it. But the burn of a blade didn't come, and she called his name, then cursed, but the sound was muffled as if someone had placed a palm over her mouth. Fueled by fury at the thought of hands on her, he whirled and put his fist into a beefy solar plexus, followed by an uppercut to the jaw with the other. His attacker went down with a thud, and he spun to Cheney.

Her arms were pinned and she was being dragged by two under-sized punks. Not that she was making it easy. One of them rattled a few words to the other, and Jonah drew a steadier breath when he heard the word, Charlsey.

Jonah waded into the fray. Cheney could have defeated a single attacker with ease. Even pinned as she was, she was already damned close to taking down one as she dealt a kick to the groin in the same moment Jonah reached for a throat.

Dragging the smaller one aside, he squeezed until the hands gripping Cheney released her arm to claw at Jonah's hands. He squeezed harder, and the thug finally lost enough air that he sagged. Jonah flung him aside then watched as Cheney finished the other.

He glanced over his shoulder at shouts from the hotel. The altercation had drawn attention from the hotel guards who were running toward them, guns drawn. He moved closer to Cheney, his gaze meeting hers, and she gave him a grin. Damn it. His heart was still pounding with terror for her, and she grinned.

When the guards recognized their celebrity guest and her companion, their faces paled. One immediately began making phone calls. The other turned his attention to their attackers, snapping cuffs of some sort on their wrists, not pulling arms behind their back but stretching them out and cuffing the wrist of one to the wrist of another until all three were linked. As the stress of his fear for Cheney ebbed, Jonah admired the ingenuity of the move. The guard apparently had only the two sets of handcuffs for three bad guys. He'd made the best possible use of them.

Hearing the wail of sirens in the distance, Jonah had the presence of mind to send a quick message to Jade before he started answering the barrage of questions from hotel security. No, they didn't know the assailants. No, they didn't recognize them. No, they knew of no reason for the attack by them. That last wasn't quite true. One of them had spoken her name. It didn't explain motive but he could guess that easily enough. Kidnapping and ransom were at the top of his list.

The hotel manager came at a trot down the center of the drive. "Shall I call for an ambulance?"

Cheney was already shaking her head and Jonah assured the man everyone was fine. No injuries.

"Maybe our staff doctor could take a look at everyone to be sure?" No manager worth his pay would want his establishment to be slapped with a lawsuit.

"No need."

"Of course. Of course." The man seemed disappointed but let it drop.

Jade and Angel were striding down the walk toward them just as a police cruiser slid sideways into the circular drive of the hotel. Two uniformed officers jumped out, carrying batons.

Between nodding at the city officers' assurances that the attack was an aberration in their city and at the hotel security personnel declarations that this had never before happened to any of their guests *ever* and ignoring Angel's glares, Jonah had a hard time appreciating the sight of their three *wannabe* kidnappers stumbling and cursing their way into the back of the patrol car with their wrists shackled to one another. Hard, but not impossible.

After Charlsey had managed to graciously accept apologies from all, the patrol car rolled away, and the security officers escorted their guests into the hotel lobby. The manager, still wringing his hands, assured them that dinner was a courtesy of the house that evening. Jade reassured him no one was hungry and they weren't checking out over the incident but a couple bottles of wine would be appreciated.

And Jonah hustled Cheney upstairs before she exploded.

Chapter Seventeen

Cheney filled the tub as high as she thought safe but water still splashed onto the floor as she slid in. The temperature was as hot as she could stand and then some. She had a few scrapes, raw places that burned where the water touched. By morning she knew she'd have a couple of bruises as well. The physical trauma didn't bother her. The emotional was a different story. That didn't soak away as the water cooled.

She grabbed a thick towel from the pile on the counter, wrapped it around her body, then another around her head. She gave up fighting the images in her mind and let them come. Better to deal with the afterthoughts now and get it over with.

When the first hand had grasped her upper arm,

she'd been more startled than anything. The touch hadn't been rough, could even have been someone who tripped while passing close and reached out to steady themselves, accidently catching her instead of a companion. Before she could turn her head, the grip had turned painful. Then her other arm was seized in the same manner. She panicked at the realization she couldn't get to the small gun strapped against her ribcage. Then anger took over.

She didn't need a gun. Close up and personal she had everything she needed in her strength and in her training, and she'd made good use of both. She'd broken at least one nose, and damaged at least one windpipe.

She hurt in places, but they'd hurt far worse, far longer. It was small satisfaction, but it was some.

She was cross-legged in the middle of the bed by the time she heard Jonah bump the connecting door, then open it before she could react. She watched as he juggled a bottle of whiskey and two shot glasses and closed the door behind him.

He stopped, his glance taking in her damp hair, before dropping to the short fleecy robe she had wrapped around her.

Clearing his throat, he said, "I have some aches and pains … thought you might have a few of your own."

She stared at him, and he stared right back until she admitted, "Yeah, fine, one or two."

He set the glasses on top of the dresser and opened the bottle, pouring generous measures into each. Then he walked back to her bed. When she didn't move, he gave her a look she couldn't decipher and sat anyway. Their legs touched, and she shifted away from him. He smiled and handed her a glass.

The silence between them soothed her. Or maybe

it was the whiskey. She handed him her empty glass. He refilled his own, but she shook her head and slid down into the covers.

"What's the other reason?" she murmured.

"For what?"

"For the whiskey, for you ... here," her throat felt tight, and she swallowed, trying to ease the constriction.

"I didn't want you to be alone. I know how hard it is for you to be constrained, to be pinned down the way those two bastards had you trapped between them."

She closed her eyes, fighting the feeling that was all too familiar. "That was a long time ago."

"Not long enough. Not for either of us."

And the memories were even closer. She fell into them when she fell into sleep knowing, on some level, that Jonah watched over her as he sipped his second glass of whiskey.

* * *

Cheney was sure Kell was dead. He would have come for her by now if he could. Quinn might not, and maybe Declan wouldn't either, but Kell would. He felt guilty because her father had died at the hands of his business associates ... if you could call the Aguilars something as dignified as business associates.

The sons were even worse than she'd thought, every bit as evil as their father had been. She'd seen some nasty characters come and go in the hours she'd been here. She wasn't sure how many hours. And maybe it had been days by now. She didn't think so, but she wasn't sure of that either. She'd slept but didn't know how often or for how long. She kept jerking awake, seeing Kell bloody on the floor, struggling to get up, struggling to get to her.

The Aguilars left her alone in this place most of the time, always with her wrists tied together, not tightly but not comfortably either. It was hard to sleep that way. They only released her long enough to go to the bathroom. And when they were gone, like now, they made certain she couldn't move at all, in any direction.

She felt pure terror when the door splintered, and the wood gave way to what sounded like the kick of a bootheel. She instinctively looked around for something to fight with, already knowing there was nothing and no way she could have even if anything were within her reach. There was nothing but the dirty blanket she slept on. She shrank backwards with nowhere to hide, no way to hide. Not the way they'd left her.

The man who stepped through took one look and lit the air with his curses. She'd never seen him before, and she knew at once he was different. She couldn't have said how he was different, but his eyes, the fury in them when he saw her told her it was so.

"Son of a bitch," he muttered, pulling a knife from his pocket. "Those low-down bastards." He'd cut the rope that had been roughly braided into her hair, then tied to an eyebolt in the wall above her. She held her breath, but he was gentle as he worked, as gentle as anyone could have been with the anger she could feel coursing through him.

When he had her free, he sliced through the rope that bound her hands loosely together. He squatted in front of her. "I have you, now, Cheney. You're safe. Kell sent me. Let's get your stuff."

She just looked at him and shook her head. "There's nothing here." No change of clothes. Nothing. She'd showered in what she wore and slept in them wet to keep from undressing. "Kell sent you?"

"He did. He wasn't sure where they had you, didn't have time to tell me all the places to look. All I knew was who, not where. Took some time to find you, and I'm sorry for that."

She tried to read his expression but she knew Kell would have come with him if he could. Didn't have time, he'd said. "Kell ... he's dead?"

"I'm sorry." And it looked like he really was.

The tears burned, but she wouldn't let them fall. One day, she'd kill them all, she thought. One day.

"We need to go," he said, and she left with him without even knowing his name. Kell had sent him. That was all she needed to know.

Before leaving California, Jonah took her back to the Flannery warehouse office to say her goodbyes. Leaving Quinn and Declan was hard.

As Quinn hugged her, she whispered, "You must kill the sons of Raul Aguilar or they will murder you just as they did Kell."

Quinn shook his head. "People like the Aguilars are never completely defeated. I'll continue to use them to help as many as I can escape them. Death would be easy. Mine is the better revenge."

* * *

Cheney woke to find herself wrapped in Jonah's arms. For a moment, she didn't move, but just sorted through her dreams, the thoughts and emotions they'd left behind. She and Jonah were both fully dressed—if her thigh-high robe counted—and they both lay on top of the covers, two good things. Bright sunlight filtered through the sheers, and that was not such a good thing.

From the angle of the rays, she judged it to be late morning. Jade wasn't going to be happy, especially once she realized both of them were missing at breakfast.

She eased from Jonah's arms and slipped into the bathroom to shower, lathering and rinsing and taking her time, standing until the water turned cool.

When she came out, Jonah was gone, and their connecting door was firmly closed. She wasn't surprised. Jonah had made his lack of interest in her clear long ago.

* * *

Jonah poured his second cup of coffee and sent Jade a message. It was a bad evening. Cheney needs a break. And it was because of yesterday's break that Cheney had a bad evening. The irony of that did not escape him.

Jade's answer was quick. She can skip the meeting this morning but the rest of us need to talk through security a final time. Construction on the runway in the ballroom started while we were out yesterday. It's almost complete. Flyers hit the street two days ago. I'd give her more time if I could. I hope you know that.

He sighed. Yeah. I know. And he did. He felt better for trying, but Cheney would be pissed if she knew that he had. He didn't plan to tell her.

He hit send and tossed the phone to the bed. After a long shower that did little to alleviate his tension, he stepped out into the hall and came face to face with Cheney leaving her room.

He tried for casual. "Jade mentioned this morning's meeting being a security run-through. Why don't you take the morning to relax?"

Cheney didn't bother to answer, just rolled her eyes and headed for the elevator. They stepped in together, rode downstairs in silence, but when they stepped out, Cheney surprised him as she turned to him with a rueful grimace. "Sorry."

"I get it," he said. And he did.

Jade glanced from one of them to the other when they entered the room, but didn't comment. Jonah considered that a small mercy.

Jade waited until those who hadn't already overdosed

on coffee stopped by the sideboard to fill and doctor their cups. Once everyone was seated, she took a deep breath. "We'll keep this as brief as we can. Hotel security is well-versed in high profile events here ... everything from movie stars to rock bands to political summits. I've talked with them extensively, and Marcus has combed through their backgrounds."

"They ... hotel security ... will be on the external doors coming into the hotel and at the inside doors leading into the ballroom. Jonah, each of their team leads has your number and yours only. They'll report any concerns, however small, to you. All have been here over a year. I'm confident we've vetted them as well as anyone could. Introduce yourself to them at the start of the evening."

"On the inside, Angel and I will focus on Charlsey. Me behind the curtains, Angel in front. Zander, as we discussed, you'll use your camera to scan the crowd, ostensibly for magazine and newspaper articles, allowing you to zoom in on any part of the room at any time."

"Lauren, managing the fashion show is all yours. Charlsey knows her part, just keep the staff away from her with any needs or questions. Whether real or pretext, she doesn't need the distraction."

Jonah listened without speaking until Jade slowed and looked around the room. "What about the incident in front the hotel?"

"A detective was here first thing this morning," Jade said with a nod for Jonah's question. "It seems the trio who were involved are bumbling local troublemakers. They keep going for a big score but never seem to get anything launched successfully. Last year they tried to break into a jewelry store but set off a series of alarms that was echoed in every storefront along that street. Apparently, the alarms in each store were linked to a central system which sounds to me like a damned good idea."

Zander frowned. "So, why weren't they in prison?"

"Because they were sitting on the sidewalk when the police arrived. They claimed to have accidently triggered the alarm by trying to see a ring one of them wanted to buy. Everyone knew they were lying—not their first offense—but nothing was taken or damaged so a few days in jail and probation. They won't get much more than that with this incident, even with their apparent motive being kidnapping with a hope of ransom."

Jonah nodded. That fit with his line of thinking. Charlsey, one had called her. Cheney's cover wasn't blown.

"Anything else? Questions or concerns? Now's the time."

No one spoke.

Jonah caught the look that Jade sent him before she turned her gaze to Cheney. "You know what to do on that runway and you know how to do it. Just before you leave your room to come down, step out onto your balcony and give a princess wave. Zander has a host of journalists and freelancers ready to take pictures and get a story to their readers."

Jonah shook his head. "No. It's too risky."

"Jonah, the Aguilars aren't here. They haven't a clue that *we're* here."

"Why take the risk?" he pushed back.

"Quit scowling at me. There's little to no risk. We need that photo op ... the skyline, the hotel sign below her ... all of it will add substance, prove she is where she claims to be when the story hits. A story that will include hints of a forced marriage when Charlsey returns home and fuel the reason she wants to escape her family. Zander has already floated that rumor in a couple of bars around town."

Jonah leaned back, still frowning, and Jade pressed her point. "When they do come for her, it won't be for Cheney. It will be for Charlsey, because she'll have asked them to smuggle her out."

Cheney looked from one to the other. "I won't stay in a bubble, Jonah." She nodded at Jade. "I'll be on the balcony. They'll have five minutes to get their photos."

Jonah cursed then sighed. "I'll be with her to enforce those five minutes."

Chapter Eighteen

Cheney stood in front of the full-length mirror and gazed at what Jade's team had created. Lauren had finished with her make-up and declared herself satisfied. Zander still tugged at her clothing here and there. Jonah stood in a corner being Jonah—silent, watchful, not happy, but quiet with whatever he was thinking and feeling. Neither was hard for her to guess.

She was in male persona for the first set. Her makeup was just as elaborate as when she would switch to female but subtly different. Her eyelashes were heavily mascaraed in black but the tips were sparkling gold. Her eyebrows were rounded instead of angled at the arch. Instead of blush, her cheeks were brushed with dark copper.

Beneath a very sheer drape of that same shade of

copper, she wore a tunic and wide-legged trousers of amethyst.

She didn't recognize herself. She was no longer Cheney. She was Charlsey.

When it was time, Lauren and Zander opened the doors, one from each side so that only Charlsey, standing directly in front of it, was visible. For a moment, the crowd was hushed. And there *was* a crowd—far more than she'd expected. The sun was slipping beneath the tree line, creating a shimmering halo through the leaves and bringing a cool freshness to the air. When Jade quietly said, "Now," from somewhere behind her, Cheney stepped out. Jonah moved quickly to close the distance between them.

Reminding herself that she was Charlsey and that appearances were everything, especially in this moment, Cheney smiled. She took a deep breath and lifted her hand in that little wave Jade had shown her, a princess wave she'd called it, first looking to one side, then to the other.

"Back in," Jonah growled at her, and she turned to go back inside. It was enough, she knew it was enough, but he'd growled at her. And, because he'd growled at her for no good reason, right at the door, she whirled back and blew a kiss. The crowd erupted into cheers and whistles.

Jonah slammed the door behind them but said nothing. Jade closed her eyes briefly but when she opened them, Cheney caught a gleam of amusement, and she grinned back. She'd needed that moment, damn it. Everything else—every damned thing, including Jonah—was out of her control but not that one moment.

* * *

Jonah watched from the wings. A part of him remained amazed that this woman who spent her life behind the scenes, a silent bodyguard skilled at fading into the background world of her client, looked completely at home as she paused, turned, flashed a smile, a pout, a flirtatious look at the blur of faces beyond the floodlights focused on her.

On their first run through, Cheney had objected to those bright lights. Jade had used every bit of her persuasive powers, and Jonah admitted they were considerable, to remind her, re-convince her, that her role couldn't be both prey and predator. Little as Jonah liked her being cast as prey, he'd had to accept it just as Cheney had.

Modeling lights were there to highlight whatever apparel Cheney had on at the time, changing the mood to match the clothing, reminding the audience that the model was as beautiful as the garment. That was critical for a realistic effect but secondary to the high-quality photographs that would be taken. Seemingly, those photos were for the purpose of launching a new designer with a new line of clothing which had hit fashion magazines across continents two days prior. In reality, those photos would be studied by the Aguilars once they were contacted with a request to provide a means for Charlsey to escape her family and the unwanted marriage that awaited her.

There were LEDs at the base of the walkway to ensure Cheney could move confidently—and safely—to the circle at the end and back. Otherwise, her safety was solely in the hands of her team. She didn't wear a weapon, and she'd never see an enemy until their hands were on her. As uncomfortable as it had to be for her, it scared the hell out of Jonah. He reminded himself the audience was select—only the most prestigious stylists, buyers, editors, and writers in the fashion industry—and by invitation only.

And Zander, by far, was not the only photographer.

Jonah felt confident, however, that he was the only one using his camera as spyware. Jonah glanced his way now and again, but hadn't, so far, seen any flash of alarm or frown of concern on the other man's face. And his phone stayed silent. He could only hope that silence indicated no cause for alarm rather than something having been missed by security personnel.

* * *

After several changes of clothing, Jade signaled for Cheney to sit for make-up alterations. Jonah leaned against a column, watching, and Cheney had to force herself to shift her attention to Lauren as she applied a line of glue above Cheney's lash line. With light, deft movements, she then placed long, fake lashes on top of the glue. Last came mascara, then eyeliner to fill in the gaps between fake and real lashes.

The curve of her brow became an arch under Lauren's skillful touch. Carmine lipstick was applied over golden brown, the effect richer somehow than red alone would have been. Diamond ear studs were exchanged for dangling emeralds. Real emeralds from a premier jeweler who would be repaid with free advertising in one of Argentina's more celebrated fashion magazines alongside Charlsey's debut performance in the country. Jade hadn't missed a trick with her plan. Everything was in place, each facet locked together with intricate precision. All any of them could do was hope those locks held as they moved forward.

Cheney felt a little more confident going into the second half of the fashion show. Oddly, not because she was now clothed as a female. Through the days and hours leading up to this, she'd discovered there was a side of her that could pretend … pretend to be something she wasn't, pretend to be who she wasn't. That kind of play had not been a part of her childhood although she'd come to understand it was natural enough for other young people. Regardless, she was comfortable simulating thoughts and feelings that weren't hers, creating them from nothing but her imagination—and Jade's.

Almost as if reading her mind, Jade exchanged a quick grin with her. "Ready?"

Cheney nodded, and it was true. She was ready, and she was confident. Jonah, however, had still not relaxed. His gaze tracked her every move and didn't ease until she made her final exit from the stage.

And then Jade threw her next curve ball. "We'll have a quick debrief upstairs then Jonah and Charlsey have candlelight dinner reservations at a Michelin-star restaurant called Celestes."

At their expressions, Jade chuckled. "Don't worry. You'll have a chaperone at a nearby table. Zander will be taking photos for the scandal rag; your story will hit early tomorrow."

"Our story?" Jonah's voice sounded ominous.

Jade gave him a look and sighed. "Let's take this upstairs while the stage is being dismantled."

Cheney gave him a look of her own and followed in Jade's footsteps.

* * *

When everyone had found a place to sit in the small sitting room in Jade's suite, she focused her gaze on Jonah and got right to the point.

"You picked lovers rather than married," Jade said.

"Eden made that choice," Jonah corrected.

"You didn't argue, and we're here. We'll plant a story of a couple thwarted by Charlsey's family who have promised her to the heir of a very old, very wealthy family. You'll be seen and photographed being very romantic this evening after Charlsey's stunning debut in Argentina. After which, her parents will demand she return home. She'll ignore them but will reach out to the Aguilars."

"How will she explain her knowledge of the Aguilars' activities?" Zander asked.

Jade took a deep breath, as she admitted, "This is where it gets tricky. Colter and I have been digging, but the Aguilars have done a good job of keeping their side business silent and invisible. We think we know a few political figures that they helped, but we're not sure enough to use those names. I think it would be sufficient if the message is very vague, friend of a friend kind of trail..." She turned her attention to Cheney. "If you can give a name of anyone that the Flannerys helped to disappear after the Aguilars extricated them from another country, that would help. A first name would be sufficient, maybe the country of origin."

Cheney leaned back in her chair, sorting through memories. "Not names. Maybe a face here and there. I'll keep thinking, but..."

She caught Jonah's frown and shook her head as he opened his mouth to protest. This was her battle. More than anyone else's in the room. She had lost more, had more to lose. His expression told her he didn't like it, maybe even disagreed, but he'd keep quiet. For now.

"We don't have a lot of time from here," Jade reminded. "In large part, this op is dependent on us moving fast. It's elaborate and it's well planned but the sooner we resolve, the better."

"No one wants that resolution more than I do," Cheney returned, keeping her voice even. "If I could recall a name, it would have to be someone I know couldn't be found or harmed if things go south." The last thing she needed, the last thing she wanted, was another death on her hands.

For the first time, since this charade began, she stood and excused herself from a meeting before it was concluded. When she reached her room, she showered then started a text exchange with Jade.

I'm not wearing makeup. Cheney didn't make it a question.

I'll tell Lauren to go light. Jade didn't make her response an option.

I'll do it myself, she persisted.

Lauren will be up later. She could almost hear Jade's insufferable calm and gritted her teeth.

She tossed the phone to the dresser and started sliding clothes across the voluminous rack in one corner of her room. If she selected jeans and a tee shirt from her dresser drawers, she knew there would be a battle so she settled for a floor-length gown of silvery white silk. The scooped neck was modest, but the gown itself was molded against what few curves she had. She'd once thought she'd rather not have had any curves. As much as her father had protected her, she'd seen and heard too much once they left the mountain. Then Jonah had come, had rescued her, had held her when she'd cried. How she felt about him—then and now—wasn't his fault but, sometimes when he looked at her, she wasn't sorry for those curves that she did have.

She was frowning at earrings, because she knew Jade would insist she wear them, when her phone pinged. She glanced at Jade's message, at least that's what Jade would call it … a message. Cheney considered it more of a warning.

Lauren was on her way.

By the time the former model knocked upon her door, Cheney was dressed, pearl drop earrings and all. Lauren's gaze swept her and, to Cheney's surprise, she smiled. "Excellent choices."

Lauren surprised Cheney further when she actually did go light on the makeup. Whether that decision was Jade's or Lauren's own, Cheney was grateful. When the other woman was done, Cheney's lids held a glimmer of pale smoke, her cheeks were dusted with the barest hint of shimmer. Against that, her lashes looked even longer, darker, and more dramatic than usual.

Standing behind her, Lauren met her gaze in the mirror. "Beautiful." That was all she said. Just that one word. Cheney smiled wistfully, and Lauren chuckled, and slipped from the room.

A few moments later, her phone sounded again. This time it was Jonah as his It's me message coincided with a light rap on the door.

She crossed the room, trying to quell unexpected nerves. This was a job she reminded herself, not a real dinner date. Nowhere near that. It was a work evening. And still her pulse jumped as she slid the lock and let him in.

His eyes widened slightly at the sight of her. He cleared his throat. "Ready? The limo's out front."

She wasn't the least sure she was ready for anything, but she nodded and lifted a small handbag from the lamp table that stood just beside the door. She slid her phone and room cardkey inside and put the strap over her head. The strap felt cumbersome but there were no pockets in the smooth line of the dress. "I'm ready." But she wasn't at all sure she wasn't lying.

Chapter Nineteen

The limo stopped smoothly in front of Celestes. The boutique restaurant was in the heart of the city and clearly popular. Cheney looked longingly at the outside seating as she exited the car but knew Jonah would never agree to that much exposure. The driver handed her out, and Jonah followed. He placed his hand at her back, and she shivered involuntarily at his touch. He slanted a look her way as the double-door swung wide. They were greeted by name ... well by Charlsey's name ... by the maître d' who led them through the small space between an extensively stocked bar and a discreet row of tables in front of a series of narrow windows.

A set of stairs at the back led to an upper floor divided into individual dining areas. Each small room had walls on either side to discreetly shield diners from their neighbors. Cheney couldn't help the soft exclamation of pleasure that escaped her when she realized their room, open to the hallway at the back, also opened to look down upon the garden seating area she'd admired below. The windowed doors stood wide to a tiny balcony over the garden. The lighting in the room was understated but sufficient for dining.

At Jonah's nod and subtle gesture, the maître d' left them with menus and withdrew, and Jonah seated Cheney himself. His let his hand slide across her back as he moved away, circling the small table to his seat opposite her. She reminded herself his attention was all part of the game … the pretense of Charlsey.

Before they had time to start a conversation, one that Cheney suspected she wasn't ready to have, a sommelier stepped into the room and handed each of them a menu of wines and mixed drinks. Cheney laid hers aside with a shrug, and the sommelier smiled and turned to Jonah who ordered. What, Cheney had no idea.

"I seemed to have made him happy," she commented.

Jonah raised a brow.

She gave a faint grin. "By deferring to the man."

Jonah snorted then surprised her by reaching for her hand across the table.

"For the spies among us?" she quipped, not quite steadily.

"And other reasons."

The words, as much as the touch of his hands and the look in his eyes, brought a warmth to her face.

"If we're lucky, Zander is the only spy," he added.

And just like that, the warmth was replaced by a chill that rippled across her back. "I thought the purpose was to be spied upon."

"By local media." He ran his thumb across her knuckles, "but they don't count. And we should still be non-existent entities as far as the Aguilars are concerned."

Distracted by the movement of his thumb, she had to force herself to focus. "Until tomorrow."

He nodded. "Until tomorrow or at least the next day by which time we'll be on our way to Rio."

The name of the place brought Layla to her mind, and she took a deep breath. "Jade said we'd board after lunch."

Jonah nodded but didn't answer as their drinks were served. Cheney took a sip from her glass and sighed. She had no idea what it was, but it was good. Not too sweet and only a hint of a burn as she swallowed. She looked up from her glass to find his gaze focused on her lips.

Only when the sommelier left, did Jonah respond to her comment. "Jade is waiting to set a firm time until she gets one of departure from the captain. They have a certain run-through of maintenance checks prior to. If they find a problem, we stay right where we are. Jade wants to leave port as soon as we're onboard."

"Concerns?"

"None really. Just a precaution."

Some of the tension she didn't realize she'd been feeling eased from her shoulders. Jonah wouldn't lie to her. He might not share everything he knew, but if he said it, it was so.

A waiter entered and took their orders.

Jonah had released her hand when the drinks were served, but he took it again and tugged her to her feet as soon as the waiter left them alone again. She retrieved her glass from the table as they walked to the balcony. The guests below them were absorbed in their food.

Most were couples with a scattering of single diners, both male and female, here and there. One of the couples was Zander with Angel, and she was surprised to see Zander's camera placed openly on the table.

When she said as much, Jonah explained, "Jade gave him fake credentials as a writer for a foodie magazine. He's allowed to take photos with the caveat from management that he publishes nothing without written permission from any diners he wants to include in the article."

"Smooth. And I guess Angel's supposed to be his date?"

Jonah gave a soft laugh. "Don't tell Angel that."

She stiffened when Jonah tugged her closer to his side and leaned his chin on her head, then realized Zander had spotted them and picked up his camera. She forced her pulse to quiet and allowed herself to relax into Jonah's embrace. All part of their story.

They stood listening to the musician in the corner of the garden until a trio of servers entered, smiling and chirping pleasant greetings. They returned to their table where one arranged dining ware and crisply folded linen napkins in front of them. Another placed their plates and saucers in precise locations. The third served fresh drinks and retrieved their empty glasses.

Already feeling the effects of whatever alcohol she'd been served, Cheney was careful to drink half her water before touching the other glass with its slice of orange floating beside a tiny straw for sipping.

After an initial sip, she looked up at Jonah in surprise. "It's different from the other." She'd expected a repeat of the flavors in the first.

He smiled at her expression and said, "I'm experimenting. Which do you prefer?"

"Both."

He chuckled and they ate, and Cheney finally relaxed altogether.

* * *

Jonah tipped their server above average when he paid the bill. Disruptions had been minimal and very discreet—quiet and courteous—throughout the evening. The conversation between him and Cheney had been easier than he'd expected all things considered. Those things being not just their current situation and the risks involved but all the things that had happened through the years and the emotions that simmered between them.

He hadn't finished his second drink, simply switched to water without fanfare. He doubted Cheney even noticed. He could hold his liquor but he wouldn't chance not being at the top of his game tonight when her safety was in his hands.

But they'd needed this. Both of them. Cheney looked relaxed and as close to happy as he'd ever seen her. He'd like to see more of that.

For the moment, he put aside the fact that their story needed this as well. The food and the wine and the images of a couple attentive only to one another. A story and photos that would be easily accessed by the Aguilars, help assure them Charlsey's request to disappear onto American soil was legitimate.

The night air was cool but still comfortable as they stepped out of the restaurant. And it was damp. Streetlamps cast pools of light through a mist to the sidewalk in front of them. Their limo was parked a few yards away on the same side of the street. Cheney gave Jonah a look when he slipped an arm around her, his hand on her waist.

"It will make a nice shot for Zander," he told her, but that wasn't why he'd done it.

Hearing footsteps moving evenly up behind them, he stepped slightly to one side, bringing Cheney with him to let them pass. In the next instant, an elbow jabbed his ribcage on the left and a second figure slid between him and Cheney on his right.

Disregarding the threat on his left, he put the man on his right in a chokehold and swung him as a weapon toward the left. Cheney entered the fight with a growl instead of staying safely to the side. When he heard her grunt as she was shoved, rational thought turned to rage. He was barely aware of Angel leaping the iron rail between the garden seating and the sidewalk, Zander close behind her.

A blinding light flashed, and Cheney cursed, shielding her face with her hands.

Before he could do too much damage Jonah heard Zander mutter, "Damn paparazzi." Jonah had just enough time to pull his punch and hook one of the camera-wielders around the neck instead. He shoved the man toward Zander who slung him to one side. Furious now, Cheney rode the other to the sidewalk while Angel put a knee in his face. Angel wore a grim smile, so Jonah stood back and let them finish the job before he shifted his attention to the photography flashes coming from the street.

Two females stood in the center, steadily flashing photographs. He strode toward them and grabbed both cameras, dashing them against the street pavers while the women shrieked in rage.

By now there were sirens wailing through the streets and staff spilling out of the restaurant they'd just left.

Jonah pulled Cheney close to him. "Are you hurt?"

"No. Are you?" When he shook his head, she twisted to check behind her. "Angel? Zander?"

"All's well."

Jonah looked irritably at the gathering crowd. "The hell it is."

* * *

The only thing that went right after what Jonah considered a damned good evening was that there were no serious injuries—unless you counted four broken, very expensive, cameras which Jonah paid for only to ensure any photographs that had been taken remained with him.

Zander had the nerve to grin at him as they left the police station after signing charges. "This is going to make a great story for Charlsey's bio."

"You do realize Jade's going to come unhinged," Jonah retorted.

Zander shrugged. "Why? No real harm done. Besides, the evening out was her idea. Hell, Buenos Aires was her idea. I got some great photos of the two of you in the restaurant. That combined with the few I got as you and Cheney smashed a couple of cameras are going to be gold." He looked plaintive for a moment. "Wish I could have gotten a few of the actual brawl, but you had me kind of busy for a minute. By the time I retrieved my camera, it was all but over."

"You might salvage the ones in their cameras." Zander brightened at Angel's suggestion.

Jonah just shook his head. He still suspected Jade wouldn't be happy.

The limo was waiting at the curb and they all four climbed in. Zander and Angel had taken a taxi earlier to set up Zander's story with the restaurant before Jonah and Cheney got there, but there was little use in doing so on the return trip to the hotel.

Jade was waiting for them in the sitting room of her suite. She eyed Cheney carefully and sighed. "At least you're okay." She looked at Jonah. "I don't like this. Cheney could have been hurt."

"You set Cheney up for this kind of attention," Zander reminded.

She narrowed her eyes at him then sighed. "Yeah. I did, but damn ..." She turned to Jonah, clearly turning over possibilities in her mind. "And you're certain those guys were who the police think they are? Paparazzi?"

"As in no connection to the Aguilars?"

"Or the two who attacked you in front of the hotel," she clarified, still looking less than happy.

"I'm sure," Jonah said calmly. "The police recognized them. Said all four—two couples—were freelancers who sold their photographs to the highest bidder. They weren't happy to lose those photographs ... apparently Charlsey is an even bigger hit than we realized ... but they were happy enough with the money I paid for them to buy new cameras."

Jade sighed. "Fair enough, and the cameras were cheap enough insurance to make sure no un-Charlsey-like photos got away from us. At this point, it looks as if the Aguilars believe Cheney was on that plane to Rio. So far, so good. Colter has someone watching them ... their every move. They've been seen at various times around town, around the docks, in and out of their homes." She looked straight at Cheney. "I don't think they'd trust anyone but themselves to come for you if they had even a clue you were here. I'm confident they don't."

Something inside Jonah eased at the words. He tended to agree with Jade on all counts. They'd have to deal with them sooner or later, but that later needed to be on their terms. Not the Aguilars.

Cheney nodded, and Jonah could tell she hadn't needed reassuring. She'd already come to the conclusion that the brothers wouldn't have hired local thugs to send after her. Easy for her, he thought, she wasn't the one worried about her safety.

Jade sighed. "I guess we just got lucky for you to be mobbed twice in less than a week."

Despite her sarcastic tone, Zander perked up. "Speaking of lucky, I can make tonight's action work for us, doubling the effect of the romantic dinner. It adds fuel to the fire for an old-fashioned, tyrant-style dad demanding his daughter return to the safety of her home. Bad enough being seen out and about and photographed on the arm of a man. Worse that the man was her rescuer in a paparazzi street brawl. Neither would look good to the non-existent fiancé." He paused, looking momentarily disappointed. "I sure hate I didn't get one of her taking that guy down."

Jade sighed and nodded. "Go for it. Any chance it can hit by morning?"

"Tomorrow is iffy, but I'll try. By the day after is a sure thing."

Jade looked thoughtful, then nodded. "Make it happen. The timing will still work if it gets to travel magazines as well as fashion slicks."

Zander nodded agreement and picked up his camera to leave. "I've got work to do. This is going to be a hell of a story. You three can hash out the rest of whatever is left."

If he hadn't been holding his camera, Jonah felt certain he would've been rubbing his hands together in satisfaction.

"What *is* left?" Cheney asked.

"Nothing really," Jade admitted. "If none of you are hurt and Zander is happy this fiasco actually occurred, I suppose we're done."

"Cheney took a gut punch."

Cheney scowled. "He got worse in return."

Jade gave her an assessing look. "I suspect taking him out of the picture maybe makes up for the other evening."

Cheney's lips curved slightly. "Maybe so." Then she nodded. "Yeah. It felt good."

* * *

Cheney lay in the dark, looking up at a ceiling she couldn't even see, wishing she could sleep. If she were home, she could have worked off this restlessness, hit some of her gym equipment or lifted weights.

Her mind kept replaying the moment Jonah had pulled her against him on the balcony in the restaurant. The moment he'd run his thumb over her knuckles. The moment she'd taken a sip of her drink and looked up to find his attention fixed on her lips.

She'd moved past all of these feelings, she reminded herself. Everything happening now was an act, and they were the actors. Nothing more. To think otherwise was to open herself to more hurt than she could bear.

It had taken long weeks to regain her self-respect when he'd turned her away, almost a woman but still only a teenager in his eyes. Weeks in which she'd avoided him, in which she'd learned to adopt a cool gaze when her glance chanced to meet his.

She'd made a life for herself with Frank's team. A good life as an integral part of the crew with co-workers like

Angel, who depended on her, just as she depended on them.

She'd moved on from constant thoughts of Jonah who'd eventually put a ring on Angie's finger. A ring that had rested on the counter along with a folded note, which Jonah hadn't read until he was alone. Cheney hated that she'd screwed up his life, his plans. Hated worse that she didn't think she'd ever feel about anyone the way she felt about Jonah Slade.

She fell asleep with those thoughts.

Chapter Twenty

Jonah drank his first cup of coffee, staring at the sunrise. After a night of dreams, he still didn't have his body under control, much less his thoughts. He hadn't planned to take Cheney to bed after plying her with drinks the evening before, but after the attack on the sidewalk, that was all he'd wanted to do. Even if it were only to hold her and know she was safe, but from the hard-on he'd awakened with this morning, his body felt otherwise.

Instead of sleep, his mind had brought memories of the night Cheney had kissed him and asked him to make love to her. He'd wanted to then, and he wanted to now.

She'd left her bed to find him when the cabin had been quiet around them, the rest of their team asleep. He'd been outside on the walkway that wrapped the cabin ... no shirt, a shot glass of whiskey and a restless mind, his gaze on the mountainside in front of him. Hearing the screen door open softly behind him, he'd turned. The sight of her in a sleep-shirt and clearly no bra, hadn't settled that restlessness.

He'd asked if she were unable to sleep and for answer she'd pressed herself against him. He'd felt her hardened nipples against his bare chest and groaned.

"Kiss me, Jonah. Please," her voice the barest hint of a whisper on the night. She'd been barely out of school, a young—very young—woman in training. Jonah had been leading the training mission that week. He'd been her superior for purposes of that assignment. Nothing could have been more inappropriate than taking her up on that offer. It wouldn't have ended with just a kiss, and he'd been smart enough to know that.

For a moment, he'd almost yielded, nearly placed his mouth on hers, open and seeking, envisioning her opening to him. With a shuddering breath, he'd stepped back. Not soon enough, he knew. Not nearly soon enough. But, hero-worship, he'd reminded himself.

Even so, temptation had never been as strong for him as it was in that moment. And now, once again. In spite of the time and distance he'd put between them, in spite of the time he'd spent with Angie, trying to convince himself they could be happy together, in spite of everything, there was Cheney. Always Cheney.

As for her ... he suspected Cheney still hadn't forgiven him for what she considered the ultimate humiliation.

Jonah thought he wouldn't sleep but he did and woke to an email from Colter to himself and Jade. The message was brief. High level meeting with Homeland Security.

Data to follow.

The data was encrypted, and Jonah felt a leap in his pulse as his code unlocked it and he began scrolling. Colter had an unerring sense of where to dig and he had dug deep.

After he'd absorbed the information, what it meant to their investigation, Jonah picked up his phone and called Colter.

* * *

Jade was waiting when they joined her in a private conference room downstairs. "There's coffee," She murmured as they came in but didn't lift her gaze from whatever was on her computer screen. "Colter has something for us."

Jonah had taken a seat while Cheney poured her coffee, so she took one opposite him and next to Jade. Zander, Lauren, and Angel filled the other chairs as they came in.

Jade glanced up, then did a double-take at Angel. "Would you please quit taking your nail scissors to your hair?"

Her expression unperturbed, Angel leaned back and finished a glass of orange juice before answering. "It needed a trim, and I don't want to go to a local I don't know."

"They couldn't do any worse," Jade retorted.

It did look a little uneven, Cheney decided, but far from hideous. But, since she preferred Jade not bring up the camel brown dye she'd used on her own hair, she held her tongue.

"Shall we get started, children?" Zander suggested.

Jade gave a huff of laughter at her own expense.

"Yes." And just that quick her expression turned serious. "Cheney, first, I have a few questions about your time with the Flannerys."

After a glance at her, then Jonah, Jade started again, holding Cheney's gaze. "You were fourteen when your dad hooked up with the Flannerys."

"Closer to fifteen by that time, but not quite there yet, so ... yeah. Fourteen."

"Do you remember how that happened? How he came to work for them?"

Cheney was silent a moment, sifting through her memories. With California his goal, they'd followed the interstate, drifting from the lake through New Mexico, across northern Arizona for the first six months after leaving the lake. They'd angled upward through the tip of Nevada and into California.

Arizona had been a series of odd jobs, mostly pulp wood and agricultural but never a place or a job where he couldn't keep Cheney at his side while he worked. She'd known he could make more money without her as part of the package, had argued she could stay alone in the places they rented during daylight hours while he worked, saying, "I'll keep the doors locked until I hear your voice. I'd open them to no one."

He'd simply look at her and shake his head. "Your Mama would weep if I failed to keep you safe."

And the conversation would end with that.

Their journey had stopped at the ocean neither of them had ever seen, air smelling of brine, and work near the docks. He couldn't work on the docks, not with Cheney, but there were plenty of odd jobs to be found day by day. Sometimes Cheney felt some of those jobs were given him *because* she was with him. Dressed as a boy in loose fitting clothing, she looked years younger than her age. Sometimes people who had little were kind to others who had less.

Pushing thoughts away, Cheney looked at Jade and started talking.

"Daddy was working for a janitorial company, cleaning warehouses. A couple of them belonged to the Flannerys."

Every night he would sweep the floors of the long aisles then use a small piece of rolling equipment to move full trash bins outside and bring empty ones inside. Meanwhile, Cheney would dust desks and file cabinets and empty ash trays in offices. Because it was after-hours work, the risk was less, but Cheney knew he kept a close eye on her all the time. She was never allowed to go farther than the sound of his voice, and he called to her often. And, because it was after hours, they might never have met any of the Flannery brothers if not for a would-be thief.

"My dad was emptying trash bins and I was emptying ash trays when a young man I'd never seen went into one of the offices. He looked around, as if he didn't want to be caught, but he didn't notice me. I watched him open a desk drawer and lift a cash box. When he took off running, I did too. I tackled him just before the door. We both had the wind knocked from us, but he jumped up first. He'd probably have gotten away if he hadn't rammed right into Quinn Flannery at the front entrance." She smiled at the memory. "Quinn held that guy with a hand twisted in his tee shirt hard enough to cut off his wind. Once the police took statements and left, Quinn took us out to eat and ended up hiring my dad. He said any man who raised a kid to do the right thing or die trying was worth his weight in gold. Not that I planned to die trying."

"And after that ... you and your dad were working

days, right? Not cleaning. What did you do and where were you during the day?"

"Quinn bought a laptop and his wife loaded it with some kind of homeschool software. Quinn told me that my job was to learn."

"Where did you study? Still close to your dad?"

Cheney tilted her head but nodded slowly, wondering where this was going. "Not always in the same office space but not far."

Apparently, Jonah wondered as well. "Where are you taking this, Jade?"

"Give me a minute and I'll get there." Jade looked as cool as she always did, but Cheney could almost feel the tension rippling through her as she shifted her gaze back to Cheney. "The people the Aguilars brought in and the Flannerys helped disappear into a better life, did you ever see any of those people?"

Cheney hesitated. "Not often and not because I was trying. Sometimes things got busy, even hectic, the Aguilars would forget I was there, and people would come and go. I'd keep my head down and pretend I didn't see anything."

"But you did." Jade said. She reached for the remote and pressed a button to lower the projection screen opposite her. "If you'll turn your chairs, you'll see what Cheney sees in front of her."

She angled her own laptop toward Cheney. "These are photos of people who disappeared from the world stage during the months that you and your father were with the Flannerys. Colter has eliminated any who are living openly elsewhere or have been confirmed as living secret lives established by our government for political reasons."

Tapping the screen, she added, "After you've looked, check one of the boxes at the top … definite yes, you saw him or her ... maybe ... definite no."

Jade leaned back in her chair, and, taking a deep breath, Cheney started with the first picture.

* * *

Jonah paid more attention to Cheney's face than he did to the screen in front of them, just checking occasionally to see if she'd checked yes, or even maybe.

An older gentleman, tall and thin with swarthy skin, silver hair, silver eyebrows. She checked no. A young woman with henna hair and green eyes seemed to stop her for a moment, but she checked no, again. A young man, little more than a teen, maybe Native American or Hispanic. After a long moment, she checked maybe. The next was a very pretty child younger than Cheney would have been at the time, perhaps twelve or so. A yes.

After she'd gone through all fourteen photos, there were three that she'd checked yes—she'd definitely seen him or her—and the one she'd checked as a maybe.

Jade quickly opened a different file. "Your responses transferred over," she told Cheney. "These are the three yeses and the one maybe but with a bio attached.

Cheney glanced at the first one and back at Jade. "The Aguilars kept bios on these people?"

"No, just the photographs with fake ID's. I guess in case they were stopped by customs when entering U.S. waters. Colter used facial recognition software to pull in their backgrounds."

With a nod, Cheney studied the photos one by one, starting with her maybe. The young man still tugged at her, and she glanced at his background information. Not Hispanic, after all. Israeli. He was the only surviving son of a high-ranking military family decimated by recent conflict. His eyes held sorrow, but she was still no more certain whether she'd seen him in her past or someone like him on a television screen, or just felt a kinship with his grief.

Her first yes had been a pleasant-faced woman with a scattering of freckles, blue eyes, and golden blonde hair. In the photo, she was dressed in jewels and furs. In Cheney's memory, she'd been simply clothed and carried an infant in her arms. But Cheney was confident of having seen her. She could almost hear the Irish cadence of her voice, and the bio matched that cadence. A wealthy Ulster wife who'd run away from her husband rather than give up her child. The child was illegitimate, but no lover in sight.

The second yes was a slightly-built older gentleman with thinning hair and a mustache more silver than black. Also wealthy, he'd been declared insane by his nephew but managed to disappear before being placed in an asylum. She could see the anger in his expression as he stared down a reporter, on either side were men in scrubs, their faces deliberately blurred.

And, then, the young girl again. She'd been gritty, that girl, angry at what had happened to her, to her family, and she'd been almost breathtakingly beautiful. Her sleek black hair pulled away from her face in a multitude of braids emphasized large, equally black eyes ... so expressive. Her father, a member of the ruling family of one of a multitude of African sovereign states—small countries—in constant turmoil, had angered the current regime. Or the regime had felt threatened by him.

The father and both sons had been killed but mother and daughter had escaped. At some point the mother had returned home, claiming the daughter died during the return crossing. Jailed as a political figure, the mother disappeared under suspicious circumstances after refusing to produce the daughter who'd witnessed the murder of her father and brothers. That state had been absorbed by another neighboring and more powerful state, but was currently struggling to reestablish itself as self-ruling entity.

On the last screen, Jonah said, quietly, "Colter is working some angles and I think we'll have more answers by the end of the day. What we know right now is that the Aguilars are, and have been, on a government watch list. Not as much for smuggling people into the country but for extortion not to turn some of them over to their country of origin."

"An ongoing source of revenue," Jade murmured.

"Exactly."

"So why haven't they been busted?" Zander asked.

"The government works in mysterious ways," Jonah quipped without humor, "but not *that* mysterious. We know they've confirmed and extricated more than a few of the Aguilars' extortion victims, many low-key government officials from varying countries who knew enough to know they were dangerous to their current government. Any who failed to pay the Aguilars risked having their children or spouses stolen and sold into slavery in third world countries. We also know they suspect there are some still out there. They want to locate, warn, and—if possible—absorb them into the fold of our government for purposes of intelligence. Once that's done, the last nail in the Aguilars coffin will be driven home. That effort has been ongoing for almost a year."

"Then Quinn disappeared," Cheney said flatly.

Jonah nodded. "Then Quinn disappeared. We have confirmation he was aiding our government with the search and a potential sting. We can't get much more out of them than that but it's something."

"So the Aguilars caught him?"

"No proof of what actually happened but strong supposition. It's likely they caught him in the act or someone—or something—tipped them off. Colter believes the Flannerys were rescuing Aguilars victims long before the government ever got involved."

Cheney stared at the wall in front of her. "With Quinn dead, Declan and I are the last people who can testify against them." It wasn't a question.

"As far as we know, that's true," Jade agreed.

"Where's Declan?"

"We don't know." Jade's response was frank but not without compassion.

Jade looked from Cheney to Jonah. Cheney saw sympathy in Jonah's eyes and braced herself for whatever was coming next.

"Colter also discovered a police report from a couple of months ago. The Flannery Warehouse offices were broken into after hours. Alarms were disabled and the entire place had been trashed ... locked doors kicked in, locks broken on overturned file cabinets, storage boxes dumped, contents scattered. We think that's when the Aguilars found the card with your aunt's address.

"An employee called in a report when she arrived for work." He paused. "Declan hasn't been seen or heard from since."

Cheney sat silent, absorbing, then lifted her chin. "Then there's hope."

No one argued, but no one agreed. She didn't care. She wouldn't give up until she knew.

Zander touched her hand across the table, then looked at Jade. "We still have a job to do, and we'll do it. What's next?"

"Meanwhile, we make the best use of this." Jade pulled up the article that Zander had written. "I don't know how you managed to get it spread so quickly, but some of the magazines actually pulled their last online issue and reposted with this."

And, with a few keystrokes, Cheney found herself staring at her image and Jonah's. His chin resting lightly against her head. Her eyes showing every damned thing she'd felt in that moment.

Chapter Twenty-one

W"hat's your idea of the best use?" Jonah asked, wondering if Cheney was going to jump and run. Her expression as she stared at Zander's article and the photographs he'd taken said it was a real possibility.

Running wasn't on Jonah's mind as he fixed his attention on the article. Zander had proven an asset in the street fight, but this was where he excelled. Every word counted, emphasizing the tight security around the mysterious young model, and every word focused attention back to the photographs. There were several from the fashion show, the male and the female Charlsey.

But the real emphasis was their evening out. The sconce lit brick walls behind a table for two. His hand reaching for hers across the table. A closeup of his thumb caressing her knuckles. Him standing, tugging her to her feet. The very real confusion in her gaze as she looked up at him in that moment. Finally standing in the dark of the street, red and blue lights flashing, while Jonah held her tucked against him.

What lay between them, still smoldering and unresolved, was a distraction for both of them. They'd get back to that when this was over but, for now, he needed her to look at him with her habitual cool distance, keeping the fire banked until they could let it burn without danger to her.

"To continue as we planned," Jade answered. "I'll send the Aguilars an email—as Charlsey—pleading for help leaving the country…escaping to America, the land of freedom. I'll attach a copy of Zander's articles. I'll express horror that my family will see this and limit my freedom even further with more than a hint that I'm in love with my bodyguard and have no desire to return home to an arranged marriage. I'll make it clear that I have no cash, that my payment will be in the family jewels I'm wearing in some of the fashion shows."

"That type payment would probably feel more realistic to them. Do you agree, Cheney?" Jonah fixed his gaze on her, wanting her to look at him, wanting her to feel in control. This wasn't her method of fighting. Her training was for stealth and strength and an accurate aim. Knowing who, knowing if, knowing when, then acting on the knowledge with split-second timing and deadly precision.

Cheney nodded slowly, meeting his gaze. "I … yeah, I think so. Charlsey wouldn't be carrying a lot of cash. Credit cards, but not cash. And she wouldn't make much use of those cards. She'd be more used to having everything paid for and managed by the very handlers she wants to escape."

"Exactly my thoughts," Jonah agreed. He shifted his

attention to Jade. "So, after you email the Aguilars, what then?"

"Unless we hear back immediately … and I don't think we will, we move on to Rio and the next venue as planned."

Angel tilted her head. "Why don't you think we'll hear back at once?"

"The Aguilars aren't stupid. They wouldn't have been this successful, survived this long, unless they were both cagey and crafty. They're going to do some digging into Charlsey, but our set up is flawless. They'll see only what we want them to see, which is a big money score with future potential for a lot more. They'll get back with us … with Charlsey in a day or two, ready to do business."

"This is what I'm sending." Jade pulled up the communication she had ready for the Aguilars. "Any suggestions for changes?"

Jonah—all of them—read in silence.

I am Charlsey. I'm currently in Argentina to model clothes. Soon, I'll be in Brazil. Morocco, after that. Then I am to return to Thailand which is what I don't want to do. My parents have promised me to a man I will not marry. I love the man with me in Argentina.

My cousin, also my friend, escaped a marriage she didn't want because your family helped her. I do have some money, not a lot as my father controls my fortune, but I have many jewels here with me. If you help me, I'll pay you with jewels or sell some to pay your fee.

My love must return to his home when I leave for Brazil, but he'll bring the jewels and meet me in America, this place California. He's not a poor man and can help pay you if the jewels are not enough.

We must hurry. When my father sees the photographs that some person took of me and wrote a story, he'll force me to come home now. I have the name of someone in Indonesia who also helps people to disappear but I want to come to the United States.

Jonah read it through and looked toward Cheney

again. Her chin was up now, and her expression held the confidence he knew she'd need to get through this.

"It's good. Enough but not too much. Charlsey sounds spoiled but not worldly, which is important. They'd be leery of someone too slick."

"I agree with Cheney's assessment," Zander said. "Anything more wouldn't ring true. I do have one suggestion to maybe add an amateurish cell phone shot of one of the photos from my article, maybe capturing my byline or the name of the slick with it."

Jade considered that and agreed, "It would be a good touch and could save them some time finding the thread to Charlsey's persona to see for themselves. Anyone else?"

"I'm not comfortable with Cheney returning alone." Only to himself did Jonah admit he was far more than uncomfortable.

"I understand," Jade agreed, "but the fact that Charlsey has a lover with money makes her a good candidate for the extortion they like to bring into play on the other side of the escape. No point in killing their golden goose or even harming her to the point that the jewels are all they get. And it's just as likely they'd consider the jewels might prove to be fakes which makes a regular payment in the future all the more attractive."

"Let me put this another way," Jonah said. "Cheney isn't going back alone."

The room was quiet as Jade leaned back in her chair and studied him. Jonah didn't look at Cheney, whose stare he could feel as he watched Jade. He couldn't read Jade's expression although he strongly suspected the glint in her eyes held more entertainment than irritation.

"Fine," she said at last, "but it can't be you. Zander was careful to keep Charlsey highlighted and you more shadowed in his photographs but seeing you up close and personal is too dicey. You and Colter are both high-profile people. You were in full view during the initial setup in Albuquerque, and we know they were watching. We can't risk having you recognized by them until it's too late."

Jonah didn't argue. The point was to get Cheney to California in safety. "Angel, then."

Angel gave a quick nod. "I like it. They'd probably anticipate a rich young woman wanting to travel with a companion, a trusted employee of the family to watch over her, but someone she trusts."

"I think they'd agree to that," Jade said, "and I think we'd all feel the better for it."

The addition didn't alleviate all of Jonah's concerns, but it damn sure helped. "Now the question is, how do you get this request to the Aguilars without suspicion? What explanation can you offer for a foreigner to have their email address even with that vague reference of them having helped a friend of Charlsey's to leave her country?"

"It will be addressed to the Flannerys." Jade said. "One of our hackers discovered that certain communications are being forwarded from the Flannerys business account to the Aguilars."

Cheney paled. "Declan?"

That, Jonah knew, would be the ultimate betrayal for her, but Jade shook her head.

"We thought so at first, but the hacking is being done from the Aguilars' end and it seems to go back to the time Quinn and his family disappeared. Whoever their hacker, he or she is good. Ours is better, and they'll send this one right along. The Aguilars will never question whether or not it came from their own hacker," she said with satisfaction.

She looked around the room, then stood. "Let's get

busy packing. We have a confirmed departure time of 2:00 this afternoon. We need to be aboard an hour before."

* * *

Cheney didn't need much time. Lauren had taken care of Charlsey's costumes and makeup. All she had to deal with were her personal items, and she'd packed most of those few things the night before. Jade had arranged for hotel staff to move the baggage from everyone's room to the limo out front. An additional SUV was packed to the roof with Charlsey's gear.

Cheney took a last look at herself in the mirror and realized she was homesick, not for her apartment but for the mountain and the lake. And, just maybe, for something she'd never had.

She walked out into the hallway where Jonah waited for her. He smiled and she accepted that the tug at her heart would always be there, regardless of what happened next or where life led her in the future.

The drive to the port was brief and very quiet. Everyone seemed as lost in their thoughts as she was in hers. The porters on the dock unloaded their baggage and carried it up the gangplank.

Angel and Jade led the way. Cheney followed, Jonah close by her side, Angel a step or two in front of them, Lauren and Zander just behind them, keeping up the pretense, the attitude, knowing someone was always watching. She and Jonah found their luggage in the same adjoining rooms. Jonah walked through her suite, checking the space, before he went into his. Their eyes met, then she closed the door behind him.

Everything was beginning to feel very much out of control.

* * *

They gathered in the ship's dining room for dinner that evening. They were a quiet group, and Cheney the quietest.

"Anything from the Aguilars, yet?" Jonah asked.

"Not yet, but the one I sent to the Flannerys has been forwarded to Aguilars' account. I suspect they'll reach out by morning."

When Cheney stood, Jonah did as well.

Jade called his name softly, and he turned. "Take care of her."

All he did was nod.

Chapter Twenty-two

Cheney stood in the shower until the water turned cold. It bothered her that she couldn't feel anything. Not fear or grief or dread. There was just emptiness.

She was shivering when she stepped back into the bedroom wrapped in one of the thick, fleece robes the cruise line provided. Looking up from wrapping a towel around her hair, she stopped in her tracks, suddenly feeling too much.

Jonah was there, propped against the connecting door, two upside-down wine glasses held by the stem in one hand and a bottle of wine held by the neck in the other.

She opened her mouth to ask him to leave, then closed it again. Most of what she felt was exhaustion. But not everything.

Jonah crossed the room and placed the wine, then the glasses, on the table beside the bed. He'd already uncorked the bottle and poured wine into both glasses. Not until he turned and walked back to the door, did she notice the covered tray he'd left on the narrow dresser near where he'd stood.

He placed the tray on the bed and removed the cover. "Compliments of the cook who realized you didn't eat much at dinner."

She eyed the chocolate éclairs "How would he realize that?"

"I happened to mention it."

She sighed, fighting and losing to every feeling she had.

Crossing the room, he tugged the towel loose and began gently rubbing her hair dry.

"Three is an uneven number," she whispered, looking up at him.

"I didn't want you eating mine, so you have two."

Tears burned her eyes. "You were supposed to have your happy-ever-after with Angie. You still can. She'll forgive you."

"She might," he agreed, "if I had any regret for what I feel. I don't, Cheney. My only regret is that it took me so damned long to realize you're all grown up."

He scooped her up and placed her on the bed, her back against the headboard. Then he handed her an éclair and a glass of wine and her heart melted.

* * *

Long after the éclairs were eaten, the wine glasses empty, and the lights were out, Jonah cradled her in his arms. She slept curled against him, so close he could feel her heartbeat upon his chest.

He finally slept and when he woke, she was in the shower, so he went to his, leaving the door open between their rooms.

She was dressed and sitting on her bed, looking uncertain when he stepped back in.

"Ready."

She nodded, still looking uncertain. He crossed to the bed and pulled her to her feet, wrapping his arms around her. He kissed her forehead, then the tip of her nose, then settled upon her mouth. When he finally drew back to look at her, she looked more dazed than uncertain, and he smiled.

"We'd better go or Jade will send the search party."

They left her room together, and when she seemed to be easing away as they walked the corridor—putting some distance between them—he closed that distance, placing his hand at the curve of her back.

Ahead of the others, they entered the dining room, where Jade sat alone. Jade looked from his hand at Cheney's back to his face. Jonah liked to think he saw satisfaction in her expression, but he wouldn't care if he didn't. All that mattered to him was Cheney.

Jade smiled. "How were the éclairs?"

Jonah gave her a look that shot daggers but when Cheney answered evenly, "Chocolate is always appreciated," he relaxed.

"Final stages, you two. Soon this operation will be a lesson for the newbies coming into the Slade Agency."

The comment gave Cheney pause. She remembered those lessons. Remembered being one of the new kids on the block. She'd known, of course, that what they'd studied in the classroom had been actual events. She'd felt the excitement of the chase, the intensity of learning the best way to deactivate a bomb, how to take down a guy a foot taller and fifty pounds heavier, how to be the fastest at determining if and when and where to aim a gun.

What she hadn't considered in her dogged determination to be the best—at least not considered enough—was what happened when an agent failed. And they did study the failures ... even more than the successes ... because what not to do often brought the most meaningful lessons.

She hadn't considered how much that agent suffered mentally when a kidnapping victim was left someplace to die and never found, as maybe Quinn and his family had been. When a hostage took a bullet through the heart or the brain or was battered to death like Lina. When the family who loved them, as Cheney loved, was left with loss and grief.

Jade must have seen something of her thoughts in her face. "How are you holding up?"

"Solid," was all Cheney said as she took a seat.

Jonah filled two coffees at the sideboard and carried them back to the table, placing one in front of Cheney. "Anything new?"

Jade gave him a look of satisfaction. "The Aguilars took the bait."

Zander and Lauren walked in, then Angel, who pulled the door closed behind her. Jade waited until they were seated before lowering the projection screen and pulling up the response the Aguilars had sent.

Our firm is willing to assist in your travel to America. It will be handled with discretion. A flight from Rio to San Francisco will be purchased in names of your choosing for you and your companion. We have found sufficient photographs to enable us to create a realistic identification for you but will need the same for your companion.

Please provide the date on which you would be free to travel and the names you would like to be known. Regards, The Aguilars

Jade gave them a few minutes then said, "I've pulled your last company photo to use, Angel. I'll need names."

"Angela Casey for me. My legal first name, my first boyfriend's last name." She grinned. "We were in eighth grade and I used to write it on the board every morning before class to make him blush."

Cheney shrugged. "Charles, I think. I'll travel in some of the male costumes. Last name Tia."

And that, thought Jonah, shot the relaxed atmosphere of the room to hell.

"Got it," was all Jade said, but her eyes held understanding.

Jonah had a different feeling. Not that he didn't understand. He did, all too well. With that choice, Cheney had just declared she was going in for the kill when the goal was a sting. He didn't like it on that level, but he wouldn't object. Not to the name or the decision. The Aguilars wouldn't connect the Spanish word for aunt with Lina Navarro, but it was a battle cry for Cheney. He glanced at Angel, who met his look and nodded.

He glanced back at Jade. "I assume you have the San Francisco PD on speed dial for when we get more information?"

Jade shook her head. "The Feds. Colter touched base with the locals but was advised that the Aguilars were under watch for human trafficking. Which, of course, we already knew."

"And it only took a decade." Cheney said with more than a hint of bitterness.

"Sooner or later, it happens," Jade said on a sigh. "One too many people get hurt. One too many go missing. One too many dies, and someone somewhere talks."

Jonah didn't let the heavy silence ride for more than a moment before telling Jade. "As soon as you get flight information, make sure Angel is seated next to Cheney. If not, get that changed. Then get me booked in a seat at the back of the plane. I want to see everyone who steps on or off that plane, pre-flight."

"And me at the front," Zander said less grimly but just as firmly.

"Might as well be all of us," Lauren said, and Jade nodded agreement.

"Might as well."

Jonah spent the rest of the day on his laptop, reading through reports, routing email, authorizing expenses, and keeping his eye on Cheney who'd withdrawn into herself. She lay on a lounge chair in the shade. Her eyes were closed, but he knew damned well she wasn't sleeping. She didn't want to talk … to him.

For the next couple of days, Jade had Cheney continue to dress as Charlsey and Zander continue to take photographs and send out promotional articles. The plan was for Charlsey to simply disappear upon arrival in Rio de Janeiro. The event had already been postponed, citing exhaustion. When they docked, Cheney would be dressed in jeans and one of the tee shirts she favored. With a broad-brimmed hat she'd blend. The team would step into a limo which would leave them at a hotel for which they had reservations for a late lunch but not rooms. Their luggage would be delivered to their rooms elsewhere.

For the next couple of nights, she let Jonah hold her, but that's all he did. It wasn't all he wanted, but it was all he did. She needed time and space, but she also needed him. It was enough for now.

* * *

The first night, Cheney slept. The second night, she dreamed. And remembered.

She had just finished the last of her history lesson, when Kell walked back into the wharfside office, closing the door behind him.

"Are you about ready for home?" Kell looked tired as he shuffled through papers on his desk, putting some in the trash, some in drawers.

Closing out the lesson, Cheney shut her laptop. It was late, and she was hungry, but she never complained. Kell took care of her. They all did. She missed her dad, but it wasn't their fault, so she always smiled at them as she did now.

"I'm ready."

"We'll grab pizza or something on the way home. Sound good?"

Her smile broadened then fled as she heard a splintering sound at the door he'd just closed. The door gave way, and the sons of Raul Aguilar stepped through.

Kell moved to put her behind him but two of them came between and held him. The third grabbed her against him. She smelled the stink of him, of food and wine and the wharf. She couldn't stop herself from gagging, and he slapped her.

As if from far away, she heard Kell cursing. The voice of the one holding her cut through. "You Flannerys think you're smart, but you are little people in a big world. We're losing money because of you. You think we don't know they go with you and their money with them. You'll pay, but that's for tomorrow. Tonight is for a different payment. Raul Aguilar took his last breath today. A life for a life. The girl belongs to us now."

Kell roared and managed to tear loose from one of the brothers, his free hand emerging from his waist with a knife. The man holding her pulled a pistol from his pocket and Cheney fought desperately to stop him, kicking and biting and clawing. The first bullet ripped into

Kell's side, the second into his chest, but he was still calling her name as she was carried out of the warehouse and into the street. And she was still screaming his name as the Aguilar brothers laughed.

"Cheney. Cheney, wake up. It's a dream. You're dreaming."

Jonah held her as she struggled. Jonah. She leaned into him, drawing deep ragged breaths of air.

"Kell," she whimpered.

"I know. I'm sorry. I know." And he rocked her in his arms until the trembling stopped. And then he held her as she fell into an exhausted sleep.

The next morning, Jonah watched as her eyes fluttered open.

"I'm sorry," she said tiredly.

"Don't be. We're going to stop them, Cheney." The words were a promise. "We're going to finish this … and them."

Chapter Twenty-three

Jonah didn't follow flight boarding protocol. He stood at the back of the waiting area, ignoring when his seating section was called in order to keep Cheney and Angel in his sight at all times. Only when their section was called did he move forward, falling in well behind them.

His gaze met Cheney's as she turned from placing her carryon in the overhead bin. Her expression eased a little at the sight of him. She took the window seat while Angel stowed her bag overhead and sat next to the aisle. Zander and Lauren were near the front of the plane on one side. Jade's seat was on the opposite in the middle.

After the first leg of the flight, Jonah relaxed to some extent. They may have been watched as they boarded, but the uneasy feeling left him once they were in the air. Even the layover was uneventful and smooth. They had time to stretch their legs and eat at a small bistro without leaving their terminal.

Cheney looked tired, but he reminded himself they all were. Even Jade was starting to wear down. He suspected every one of them appeared a little ragged when they finally emerged from San Francisco International in the late afternoon hours. Assuming they were watched at this point, Cheney and Angel walked together, speaking to no one. The remainder of the group kept them in sight from a distance and at different angles.

Three spotless SUVs waited for them at the baggage claim exit, and they traveled in pairs. Jade had booked them into the nearest convention hotel as restauranteurs. The top floor was a convention suite with a private elevator which could be locked by the occupants. It was the first thing Jonah did.

Jade called for a quick debriefing in the dining room where they found heavy hors d'oeuvres, chilled wine, and a fully stocked bar.

She sank into a chair with a sigh and looked at the plate she filled. "I may be too tired to finish all this. But not this," she added, lifting her martini glass.

"Colter will join us first thing in the morning. Tomorrow, we wait. The next day we move."

Angel frowned. "What are we waiting *for*?"

"The Feds. Colter is going to brief us, and we'll put our game plan together, but it has to mesh with whatever the Feds have in mind. They know they need us ... Cheney is a key witness."

"I don't like it," Cheney said tightly.

Jonah wasn't sure he did either, but he'd hold his thoughts until they heard from Colter.

"You're ... we're ... all going to crash shortly and we'll need tomorrow to rest, regardless. We can't go into this on fumes and anger alone. And we're all angry. On this floor, behind the locked elevator and locked door, there's a gym in the northwest corner and a sauna in the northeast corner. There's also a mini-library with everything from political rags to the latest novels. The conference room doubles as a dining room, and a chef will be here at 8:00 a.m., so we'll have all we need throughout the day. Oh, and your bags are in your rooms, no particular room assignment." Her gaze went to Jonah as she spoke, and he lifted a brow. "If you don't like where you are, pick another. There are several standing empty."

When he found that his room adjoined Cheney's, he silently wished Jade a good night. The connecting door stood open. Cheney's luggage was on the floor, her shower running.

He was at a small desk tucked into one corner when he heard the door close quietly, but no sound of the lock turning after. He wanted nothing more than for Cheney to rest, but if the nightmares came, he'd be able to get to her.

* * *

Cheney hit the gym before daylight, then the jacuzzi and the sauna. Breakfast came last. The chef had just arrived and was asking preferences in the dining room when she walked in. Jade and Jonah were there with Colter but the others seemed to be taking Jade's suggestion of rest to heart.

Cheney had, as well, but hers had been in the form of deep sleep. Lying in one place for any amount of time after waking was a form of torture for her. The gym and the jacuzzi had helped.

Colter rose from his chair when she walked into the room and gave her a hug which felt reassuring, but odd. She wasn't, never had been, a hugger. Few of the family greeted each other with more than a nod, maybe a smile … at least not at meetings, which was when she saw most of them. But she hugged him back and took a seat, smiling at the chef who came to stand beside her. He made several suggestions and just shook his head when she told him she'd have whatever anyone else was having.

"That didn't go over well," she said with a smile at Jade.

"No worries. He'll bring what he wants you to have, and I'm sure it will be excellent."

That proved to be the case, and she was finishing the last bite when Angel walked in looking as if she were on vacation. The other three soon followed.

Cheney was getting restless by the time everyone had eaten, and Jade was ready to get to business.

Jade lowered a projection screen and displayed a diagram of a portion of the San Francisco dock and two long warehouses, side by side. Cheney fought a sweep of nausea as memories swept her. She could smell the brine. She could also smell the blood. Her father's and that of Raul Aguilar and then Kell's. But she kept her chin up, and her eyes open. Jade was right. It was time to end this. All of it.

Colter got to his feet and walked to the screen with a pointer. He touched the end of the space between the warehouses. "The Aguilars want to meet here." He looked at Cheney. "They want you to come alone tonight after dark, with the jewels, in a rental car, and park it at the end away from the water. This would allow them to force you back into that rental car and drive you to a place of their choosing. Or push you into either of those side doors leading into the warehouses themselves. Or push you toward the waterside and onto a boat."

"And that," Jonah said with an edge to his voice, "is not how this will go down."

Colter gave him a look, half-smiled, and said, "No, it won't." He refocused on Cheney. "Jade has responded that the rich boyfriend—rich enough to pay ransom, if they were smart enough to pull this off—won't arrive in San Francisco until tomorrow evening. He'll drive Charlsey to the docks from the airport and they'll park at the end of the warehouse as requested."

He touched the side door of first one, then the other warehouse. "The Feds have been working this long enough to have undercover agents in place as dock and warehouse workers. As soon as the Aguilars show themselves on the outside, they'll have an agent inside each warehouse, at these doors. Zander and Angel will be in the front seat of the car and park where requested. They'll get out. Jade and I will be in the back seat and stay out of sight, until needed."

He pointed at the dock. "Cheney, you and Jonah will arrive on a skiff and wait at the water end of the warehouse until it's go-time."

He sent an unsmiling look around the room. "Personally, I'd prefer to let the Feds take this one. Jade said no." He looked straight at Cheney. "She said you needed this."

Cheney watched Jonah place the pen in his hand carefully on the table. She lifted her gaze to his scowl and waited, as did everyone in the room. After a moment, he took a breath and looked at Colter. "Keep going."

"We anticipate only the three brothers," he said focused on Jonah now. "As Cheney said, they trust no one but themselves. Everything the Feds have seen so far, confirms that. More, they've eliminated every enemy who has ever crossed them so they're arrogant. Zander with Angel, who'll be dressed as Charlsey, will walk forward to meet the Aguilars. As soon as the brothers step out of the car, Jade will alert you and Cheney to leave the skiff and move in behind them. We can't predict where the Aguilars will choose to position themselves, whether center of the warehouses or closer to one end or the other so you'll have to play this by ear. And this is where it all has the opportunity to go south. Remember, we have their email. We have Cheney as an eye witness to the murder of Kell Flannery. We have what we need to convict and jail them. We just need to take them down. The Feds prefer them alive, but …" He shrugged and stepped away from the screen. "Questions?"

There were none.

They met over dinner that evening, reviewing every move a second time. This time Jade led the discussion … and there were still no questions.

Colter had one last thing to say, and he was even more blunt than before. "The Feds may want them alive. We don't care. If it comes to it … and I'm certain it will … Cheney and Jonah, take out the furthest on your left and then next to furthest. Whoever else is in the fight, take the Aguilars on their right. No need to take a man down twice and let one walk free."

* * *

Jonah stared up at the ceiling in the dark, envisioning all of the things that could go wrong the next day. He couldn't do what he wanted, which was pull rank and insist that Cheney remain here surrounded by Feds protecting her. As much as he wished, he *wouldn't* do that to her. She'd earned the right to play her part. She wanted it, and she deserved it. But the thought of something happening to her was eating him alive.

He felt certain she'd fallen asleep long ago, hoped she had, wished he could. He punched his pillow then froze at a sound from her room. The connecting door opened quietly, and he waited, aching with wanting to hold her. He turned on his side, wanting her to know he was awake, and she came to him, slipped under the covers and into his arms.

Jonah wrapped himself around her, and they both slept.

* * *

The Flannery warehouses were not on the bright and shiny end of the docks. Not the thriving, lucrative end. The water smelled as nasty as she remembered, or maybe it was the clothes Jade had unearthed for them which fit their surroundings. Cheney wore faded jeans and a chambray shirt over a gray tank top. Jonah wore khakis Jade had probably found in a secondhand shop and a work shirt that had seen better days. Despite the moonlight, it was just dark enough that their disguises would pass scrutiny.

The skiff was nondescript but solid and tied right where Colter had said it would be. Jonah untied the knot, and her pulse raced with anticipation. Today was the day that old debts would be paid … her father's death and Kell's, Quinn and his wife and their children. Her prayer, there, was that the children hadn't suffered. She hoped Declan lived still, but knew she'd likely never know. The Aguilars had left him with no reason to come back here.

Jonah let the boat drift from the far end of the canal, past buildings that had seen better days. Now and again, he touched an oar to the dock to keep the skiff from banging against it. The water barely rippled with their passing. There were fishing poles and a bucket of bait at their feet. They could have been any couple looking to catch an evening meal or just get on the water and away from whatever waited at home.

Her heart thrummed in her chest as he used the oar to slow to a stop behind the warehouse closest to open water. She could barely make out the weathered sign on the front. Flannery Warehousing. Memories haunted her as Jonah retied the boat to the dock and laid the oar quietly in the bottom.

Then they waited. The dock remained deserted.

When Jonah lifted his hand without looking back, she took a deep breath, releasing it slowly and quietly as she slid out of the chambray shirt. He signaled her to loosen the single wrap that held the bow of the boat in place. She peered over his shoulder as he edged the side of it against the dock. When she stepped out, Jonah followed, then gave the boat a push, letting it drift backward so that it didn't bump the dock.

Between the warehouses, the Aguilars waited for their prey, their backs to the water. A chill rippled through Cheney at her first glimpse of them.

Jonah's hand brushed Cheney's cheek before he pointed to the back of the warehouse closest them. He crossed in the open and without haste toward the back of the other. Cheney moved into place then held her breath through Jonah's every step. If any one of the Aguilars turned, he would be seen. None of them did.

Cheney thought she could see Angel and Zander walking away from the car, toward the Aguilars. Unless something had gone wrong, it had to be them. As they came closer, she could see the gauzy, voluminous trousers that Charlsey had worn on stage. Angel's hair had been dyed the color of a fox's tail even to the white tips.

All three Aguilars stood waiting, slightly apart from one another, free to move, free to fight, free, Cheney thought, to die.

Jade's voice came through the earpiece to both of them. "Jonah, Cheney, take your shots. Angel, be ready when you hear the first shot fired."

* * *

Jonah looked at Cheney across the space between the two warehouses. They both were at good angles, giving them equal opportunity. Either could make the perfect shot. Either could die. Taking a deep breath, Jonah gave Cheney what he knew she craved. As she watched him, he signaled a one-two punch by holding up his fingers. Lifting his pistol, as if to tap the metal siding next to him on one, and pointing to her on two.

Cheney nodded and raised her pistol between both hands, prepared to step out. Then Jonah did just what he'd mimed. He tapped lightly on the metal, not loud but enough to distract either Aguilar, to make one turn. And one did, but neither his turn nor his reaction was fast enough, Cheney swung out and fired, aiming for his gun hand. Her bullet exploded flesh and bone and gunmetal. He screamed, dropping to the ground and rolling in agony. He'd live to stand trial, and the Flannery tattoo on Cheney's arm gleamed in the moonlight.

Jonah's bullet hit the femoral artery in the second man as he froze in place, staring at Cheney's tattoo. Someone might stop the flow of blood to save his life. It wouldn't be Jonah.

He shifted his attention to the third Aguilar. Angel stood with her knife still in hand, watching as he toppled forward to the ground. Blood welled from the bullet hole in his back. Jonah spun and lifted his gun as the man who'd fired that shot walked up behind the brothers.

Cheney tensed and turned in sync with Jonah's movement, finger on the trigger, then her eyes widened. "Declan," she whispered and started walking, then running. He caught her against his chest when she flung herself at him.

* * *

Officers swarmed from inside and atop the warehouse. Their lead looked from the wounded to the dying to the dead. "Didn't leave us much to do but clean up the mess."

"Problem?" Colter asked, walking up, Jade beside him.

"Not for me. All I have to do is send a cleaning crew out. The city is used to paying that bill." He tipped his hat back. "I'll be in touch for a statement from each of you. I expect you'll want to get that out of the way and head back to New Mexico."

"The sooner the better," Jonah said, keeping an eye on Cheney who looked fine with the damage they'd done.

They shook hands and parted, leaving the Marshals to call for medical assistance and local PD backup to secure the scene.

Declan returned to the hotel with them and sat next to Cheney, listening quietly as Jade led a final analysis of the operation. Jonah suspected Declan wouldn't have been much older than the teenaged Cheney when she and her father had arrived in California. And in all likelihood, he was as alone in the world now as she'd been then.

Pulling his thoughts from the man, Jonah gauged the mood of the room. They'd accomplished what they'd come here to do but there was no sense of elation. Relief, yeah, that there were no casualties on their side. Some satisfaction for a critical job well done.

And one complaint as Angel slanted a look toward Declan. "That was a hell of an aim, Flannery ... but it was supposed to be a blade instead of a bullet. My blade."

Declan matched her look for look. "I won't apologize, but I'll thank you for the compliment."

Angel grinned at the comeback and leaned back in her chair with a look of satisfaction.

"Of course, we all regret that the Aguilars turned violent," Jade brought their attention back to her with the smooth lie recorded on the device in front of her. "A peaceful capture would have been preferable to us but apparently not to them. Regardless, the locals and the feds have been made aware that you were part of this op from the beginning, Declan. Our attorney will be present as each of us give our statements."

Jonah saw Declan shoot Cheney a questioning glance. When she tipped her chin at him, he nodded at Jade. "I'll thank you for that."

"We have a place for you in New Mexico," Colter said from the other side of the conference table. "Just say the word."

For a moment Declan didn't speak. "Maybe," he said slowly. "Maybe, but not yet. I've things to do here. Someone knows where Quinn and his family are buried.

I've no hope they're alive, but I'll find them and I'll bring them home."

Jonah felt as much as saw the shudder of grief that went through Cheney at Declan's words. "Someone will be assigned to work with you on that," he told Declan. "I'll have them here by morning."

Again, Declan nodded acceptance, this time without speaking.

* * *

Cheney curled beside Jonah in the dark, more than ready to step on that plane the next day. She kept seeing the look on Declan's face, the initial doubt, the slow belief that someone cared enough to help. The look at her for confirmation of that belief. At long last, she'd been able to do something—not enough, but still something—to return to the Flannerys what they'd done for her all those years ago.

She thought Jonah was asleep until he said quietly, "I know your father is buried here in California. I think it's time for him to be home, again, back on the mountain."

Tears burned her eyes as he gathered her close, but they were good tears. The past couldn't be changed but sometimes, just sometimes, wrongs could be righted.

Chapter Twenty-four

Cheney lay back in the shade, staring at the canopy of trees above her. She could hear the occasional splash of a lure hitting the water below. The mountains around her seemed to whisper, carrying the sound through the trees and the leaves and the water.

Two days ago, they had collected Lina's ashes from the crematory. Jonah had thought Cheney would want a memorial, a service to celebrate her aunt's life with friends and family, but all Cheney had wanted to do was bring her home to the mountains to rest near her best friend, Cheney's mother.

From the graveside, they'd come here, to the Slade cabin, although cabin was a misnomer. It wasn't grand but it *was* large and rambling. She could imagine it filled with family. She glanced at the ring on her finger. *Her* family. The thought made her smile as she heard Jonah make his way up the rocky slope from the clear stream below.

Acknowledgments

Many thanks are due airline pilot, friend, and family member, Russell Blackwell who provided, not just the logistics I needed to know for my bad guys to crash a private plane over the jungles of Brazil, but the most effective way to cause that crash realistically.

And the same appreciation is due boat captain, Tim Armand, for all the logistics needed for my good guys to reach their South American destination by cruise ship. He kept me out of trouble with information I didn't know enough to know I didn't know. Tim also had the good sense to marry someone very dear to me. Such a smart guy!

Not least by any means, I'm forever grateful to Rebecca Barrett who helped me untangle the messiest plot I've ever conceived. And, a huge thank you to my beta readers: Amy Connolley, Donna Townsend, Georgia Ryle, Eve Osborne, Dawn Hasiotis, Sharon Hurley, and Tammy Baughman.

Despite these acknowledgments, any mistakes remain mine.

* * *

Thank you for taking the time to read *A Dangerous Charade*. If you enjoyed it, please consider telling your friends or posting a short review. Word of mouth is an author's best friend and is much appreciated.

Thank you,

Susan

Also by Susan Yawn Tanner
The Bellamys of Texas historical series:
Winds Across Texas
Fire Across Texas
Storm Out of Texas

The Bellamy Legacy contemporary series:
A Dangerous Inheritance
A Dangerous Charade

New editions from Secret Staircase Books
The Scottish Highlands Romances
Highland Captive
Captive to a Dream
Exiled Heart
A Warm Southern Christmas
(a historical romance novella)

The Cat Callahan Mysteries
Callahan and the Horses of Hope
Callahan Goes Rodeo
Callahan in Action
A Callahan Christmas (short story)

Visit Susan's website to discover more about the
author and her books. Sign up for her newsletter where
she announces new books and exciting giveaways.
https://susanytanner.com/